THE RESISTANCE PROTOCOL

WORKS BY TY'RON W. C. ROBINSON II

<u>BOOKS</u>

DARK TITAN UNIVERSE SAGA

MAIN SERIES

Dark Titan Knights
The Resistance Protocol
Tales of the Scattered
Tales of the Numinous
Day of Octagon
Crossbreed (Forthcoming)
Heaven's Called (Forthcoming)

SPIN-OFFS

In A Glass of Dawn: The Casebook of Travis Vail
Maveth: Bloodsport (Forthcoming)

COLLECTED EDITIONS

Dark Titan Omnibus: Volume. 1
Dark Titan One-Shot Collection
The Swordman Collection
The Commander Norland Collection
The Chosen Son Collection
The Nano Man Collection

THE HAUNTED CITY SAGA

The Legendary Warslinger: The Haunted City I
Battle of Astolat: A Haunted City Prequel (KOBO Exclusive/Forthcoming)
Redemption of the Lost: The Haunted City II (Forthcoming)

OTHER BOOKS

Lost in Shadows: A Novel
Lost in Shadows: Remastered
Accounts of The Dead Days
The Book of The Elect
Hod
Hallow Sword: Cursed(KOBO Exclusive)

ONE-SHOT STORIES

Maveth, The Death-Bringer
Mystery of the Mutant-Thing
Shade and Switchblade
Retribution of Cain
The Mythologists

TY'RON W. C. ROBINSON II

CONTENTS

HALLOW SWORD
THE UTOPIA CONSPIRACY

I

BURIED DEALINGS

Light of the moon shined down with silence covering in the streets of Retropolis. *The Rapid-Blade*, sped down the deserted streets like a lightning bolt through the clouds. The Swordman himself, is heading towards a secure warehouse after receiving word the crime lords, Elliot Slade and Ramon Lamono Carr would be having a meeting. A beeping sound erupts from a screen inside the vehicle. He looks at the screen, it's Allison, contacting him. He presses a button to speak with her.

"What do you have?"

"I have more information concerning the meeting between Slade and Carr."

"I'm listening."

"The two are meeting to discuss some idea of a utopian Retropolis. In their own words. Didn't you talk about something like this before?"

"It's called The Utopia Conspiracy. It's been going around the rumor mill within the lower areas of Retropolis for months. A plan to completely bankrupt the city and herald it into chaos, where only Slade and Carr would pick up the pieces and create their version of order out of chaos they would create."

"What do you intend on doing about it, beloved?"

"I plan to cease it."

The Rapid-Blade passed by a sign which read, "*Thank you for visiting Retropolis.*" Later passing another street sign saying, "*Welcome to Mass City, the Sister City of Retropolis.*" He continues to speed down the streets into Mass City, with civilians looking out of windows, staring at the vehicle with suspense. The Swordman drives further, seeing a warehouse in the horizon. He also notices a set of cars parked nearby the warehouse.

"I have found the warehouse. Keep in touch in case I contact you."

"I understand. Be careful."

Allison turned off her signal as The Swordman stops the vehicle. He exits. Once out of the vehicle, he reached in and raises up the Sword of the Elohim, placing it onto his back. He stealthy approaches the warehouse. Spotting the cars, he takes a glance at the license plates.

"These vehicles belong to their men."

Instantly knowing they belong to Slade and Carr's henchmen. He gazed around the warehouse and raises up his right arm, from his gauntlet fires a grappling dagger-hook, which pulls him up from the ground to the top of the warehouse.

Inside the warehouse sits over a dozen henchmen, some standing by the entrance points, others are sitting down at tables drinking beer and playing cards. Sitting together at one table is both Elliot Slade and Ramon Lamono Carr. The two of them drinking beer, smoking cigars, and talking amongst each other.

"So, what do you think about the idea of moving the plan ahead?" Slade asked. "You know, to keep things going at a faster rate?"

"I personally believe we should take our time on this. Because, once we bring about the whole bankruptcy of Retropolis deal, it will take some little time before the people cooperate with us and follow suit with our plan."

"Why would we wait for them to cooperate with us? This is my solution, we bring in the ones that side with us and we kill the ones that don't. A simple plan. A simple solution."

"Ok. But how would you handle this "Swordman" fellow they speak about?"

Slade laughs at the mention of The Swordman.

"You're talking about that myth. Ramon, The Swordman is nothing more than a folklore passed down through the generations. Hell, even the Retropolis Police Department don't believe in some Knight of Faith cleaning up their streets and doing their own work."

"But, you heard about the guy taking down that woman a few weeks back. The one with the car."

"I only know about the woman. I hear she's as crazy as they come."

"Wouldn't want to look her in the eye is all I'm saying on that subject. It's best she stays in Pegasus."

The lights of the warehouse flicker. The flickering gets the attention of Slade, Carr, and their henchmen. They slowly reach for their firearms as they make moves towards the entrance points.

"Who's playing with the damn lights?!" Slade said.

The lights shut off for a short period of time. The henchmen stand still with their guns pointing to all entrances to the warehouse. Slade and Carr stand still nearby one of the exits.

"Whoever thinks this shit is funny, I suggest you turn the damn lights on and reveal yourself to us." Carr said. "We don't have time to play games."

After three seconds, the lights flicker on and standing in the middle of the floor is The Swordman, staring a hole through both Slade and Carr. They stand in fear of The Swordman, as if they're looking at a ninja crusader with only his eyes visible to their sight.

"So, you truly exist!" Slade said.

Both crime lords command their henchmen to run over and attack The Swordman. The henchmen follow the order and ambush The Swordman, using their fists and feet to knock him to the ground. He shoves as many as he can off him and fights them off with a set of martial arts techniques and kicks. He grabbed one henchman by his throat, slamming him through one of the wooden tables.

"Don't just stop there, guys!" Slade yelled. "Keep at it with him!"

Another pair of henchmen run, he releases his grappling hook toward them, pulling himself closer as he clotheslines them, one after another. He stops on the ground, reaches into his belt and starts throwing shuriken in the shape of swords and daggers at the henchmen, connecting and piercing them in their chest, sides, and even necks. After some of the henchmen are down, he reaches to his back, pulling out his sword. The few henchmen standing surround him.

"It's best you leave the building." He said. "Otherwise, you won't be getting out alive.

The henchmen lunge toward him and he begins to kill the henchmen with the sword. Slade and Carr can only stare at The Swordman as he finishes off the remaining henchmen. Slade held his arms out, his cigar falls to the floor. This is not what he expected the night to be.

"You just killed most of our men." Carr said. "I thought they said you were some sort of hero."

"Not a hero of your understanding." said The Swordman.

The Swordman begins to approach Slade and Carr, the warehouse doors burst open and standing at the entrance is a man wearing a gray suit and a black mask that resembles a skull. The Swordman turns and stares at him.

"Slade. Carr. I thought we had a business to discuss." The masked man said.

"You can state your business with me." The Swordman declared. "Who are you?"

"My, my. So, the folklore is true. This is The Swordman that I've heard about in my youth. The myth that which my men tremble when they hear your name. So, that would mean the story of your sword is true. That sword comes directly from The Creator."

"You didn't answer my question."

"Oh. Mr. Swordman, from now on you can call me Sir

Onyx."

"Sir Onyx. It looks like you're going to be joining Slade and Carr on a trip Rockward Penitentiary."

Sir Onyx laughs hard. Rubbing his chest.

"I'm not going to Rockward, Dark Cavalier. I still have much business to do while I'm out and about."

"You don't get to make the decisions anymore."

"I still do."

From both sides of the warehouse and from the back enter three men. Dressed in clothes similar to the henchmen, but well-dressed. They slowly circle The Swordman. He stands his guard with his eyes locked on Onyx.

"You really believe three men and handle me."

"No. I believe they can buy us some time to escape."

The Swordman turns around, catching Slade and Carr running to the exit. He ran after them, caught off guard by a punch to the face from one of the three men. Onyx laughs at the sight of it.

"This is good. Well, Mr. Swordman, I'll leave you to The Party People. Do what you will with him, boys!"

Onyx leaves the warehouse and only The Swordman and The Party People remain in a sea of unconscious and dead henchmen. The Party People, named as Trystan, Charles, and Jordan are pumped up with energy and show their excitement to be facing The Swordman.

"This is what we've been waiting for." Trystan said. "To get our hands on someone like you."

"Yeah." Charles said. "We wanted a shot at that guy in

Enigma City, but we couldn't match his power level."

"So, you'll have to do." Jordan said.

From one of the doors comes a man moving swiftly into the warehouse. He takes out all three of The Party People with a succession of blows to the head in quick succession. The Swordman watches them fall to the ground, looking at the man, who has black hair down to his shoulders with facial hair and sideburns, wearing sunglasses and wearing all black clothing. On his shirt is a stylized letter "T", designed to appear as a carved skull. The Swordman stares at the man.

"You took them out in approximately one hit in a matter of seconds." The Swordman said.

"Because I know these men very well. They're from my territory and now you'll have to do for me."

The Swordman raises up his sword as the man removes his black trench coat, pulls out his own sword from the coat.

"By the way, the name is John Terror. I've always wanted to meet The Swordman. Was curious to see if the legends were true."

"Prepare yourself to find out."

"I already have."

II

A SPIRITUAL ASSASSIN

The Swordman and John Terror clash their swords together. Having a test of strength to see who will hold their own against the other. Terror grins at The Swordman, who's eyes are locked on Terror. The swords continue to scrap against one another. The Swordman swiftly moves and elbows Terror in the head. Terror drops his sword as The Swordman lunges toward him and slamming him on the ground. Standing over Terror, The Swordman places his foot on Terror's neck and stares at him.

"I've seen your emblem before. You're the spiritual assassin from Chicago."

"Am I supposed to be impressed by your knowledge of the lands? Because I'm not."

"You have this moment to tell me why you're up here in another country."

"Take your foot off my throat and I will tell you why I'm here."

The Swordman goes to remove his foot before stomping

Terror in his chest. Terror holds his chest, rubbing it to ease the tension.

"Don't try anything or you'll be the one slain this night."

"Good luck with attempting it."

Terror gets to his feet, placing his sword back into a sheathe that's connection to the interior of his trench coat. Putting the coat on, The Swordman stands still, waiting for Terror to explain his appearance.

"You see, those three guys that attacked you. The Party People. I've been on their trail for a few weeks now. That's what brought me up here."

"So why would they be allied with this Sir Onyx character if they're from your territory."

"I've never heard of a Sir Onyx nor have I seen him in Chicago. But, since they work for Onyx, I will assist you in stopping him. Even though I work better alone."

The Swordman nods. He knows what it means to work alone.

"I can respect that. You can aid me in finding Sir Onyx and bringing him to his end along with his business associates."

"It's fair enough."

"Once we stop Onyx, it's your job to take these Party People and anyone else from Chicago from this place before the officials do. Return to your territory to avoid further incidents."

"That supposed to be an order?"

"It is an order."

The Swordman walks out of the warehouse and back to the Rapid-Blade. He enters it and drives away as Terror looks onward and looks back at the bodies lying on the ground around him.

"Nice car." Terror said with a hint of a smile.

The following day, the Retropolis Police Department are visited by the Mayor of Retropolis, Charles Baker who's come to talk with the officers and Commissioner Austin about the rumors circulating of The Swordman's existence. Baker enters the department, seeing the officers facing him. They pay their respects toward him and he can see it. From one of the corners walks Austin, wearing a khaki trench coat, he takes it off and places it on the back of a chair.

"It's good that I speak to all of you at one time." Baker said. "That way, it'll sink in the better."

"Mayor, if you don't mind us asking." An officer said. "We know you've heard about this "Swordman" legend, but none of us have actually encountered him."

"I suggest you do. The Swordman myth has been around for centuries. Formally called a Creed of Swords with more than one Swordman throughout the annals of time."

"But what of that man in Enigma City? The one that flies?" Another officer said. "Or what of that metallic man in Jersey with the nanobots?"

"They are not our concern. We live in Retropolis. Not Enigma City nor Newark, New Jersey."

"I got you, sir."

Austin holds his hand up, gaining the Mayor's attention. Baker looks at him and points to him.

"Yes, Commissioner."

"How do you suggest we handle this "Swordman" problem?"

"By any means of force. I'm sure with the men and women at your disposal, Commissioner Austin, you can find a way to capture him and bring him in to justice."

Austin nods slowly. Yet, unsure.

"What happens if we come across him and he refuses to cooperate?"

"You do what needs to be done."

Baker thanks them for their short time and leaves the department. Austin returns to his office where Detectives Justine Copeland and Cash Hankinson follow. Austin sits at his desk as Justine and Cash enter the door. Austin's office walls are covered with crimes that the department have succeeded in. On the wall behind Austin is a poster with the title, *"Does The Swordman Exist?"*.

"Commissioner, I believe that you should let me, and Cash find The Swordman."

"Why is that, Detective?"

"Because we've seen the car he drives, and we know what brings him out in the open."

"What do you have in suggestion?"

"What if, we let that woman out of Pegasus." Cash said. "You know, put her out on the street. Her presence alone will grab The Swordman's attention."

Austin stares at Cash with confusion. He shakes his head slowly. So does Justine.

"May I ask who brought you into this force, Detective Hankinson?"

"I come from Enigma City. But I was transferred here. They said Enigma couldn't handle my way of doing duty."

Austin nods while clicking his pen.

"I can see why they would."

"Anyway, Commissioner. Let us handle The Swordman and we'll do the job right."

Austin sighed. Putting the pen down.

"Very well. But, Justine, keep an eye on Cash here. I believe that if you come into conflict with The Swordman that Cash could be a problem."

"I'm standing right here, Commissioner."

"I know. That's why I told Justine what I just said."

"Thank you, Commissioner." Justine said as she and Cash left Austin's office.

Austin gets up from his chair and turns back, facing The Swordman poster. He keeps his gaze on the poster for about ten seconds before returning to his paperwork on the desk.

Downtown in Retropolis at the Cherub Enterprises, Kenari approached his main office, scheduled to a meeting with two of his associates, Jacob Blake and Steven Cobb. Exiting the elevator, he walked down the hall of the large building. He looked to his left, seeing the associates sitting in his office. Blake wearing his casual suits and clean-shaven looks and Cobb dressed a t-shirt and jeans with a blazer with his wavy hair standing out. He enters his office calmly as the associates see him and immediately stand up.

"Welcome back to Cherub Enterprises, gentlemen." Kenari

said. "Good to see you once more."

"It is a pleasure, sir." Blake said. "We have great news to discuss with you concerning your suit and vehicle."

"I'm already waiting to hear it."

"Better yet, we can show you."

They leave the main office and head to the lower parts of the Enterprises building where it's covered with weapons across the walls. They enter the weapons room, walking towards an area that looked to be an open closet. Blake presses in the password to the closet door and it slowly turns, revealing The Swordman suit.

"May I ask of the improvement that you've done?"

"I've taken the measure of enhancing your suit's layer of armor. I've added a little more plating to it to avoid possible attacks from knives and it also produces some counter measure against gunfire."

"I could've done this myself you know."

"Sure. But I don't know if you thought about the idea of using one of the rarest metals in this earth."

"Which one are you preferring?"

"Thanks to some of your fellow swordsmen brothers in the east, we've come to have a small set of quakerium in our possession."

"Quakerium. Seriously"

"Yes. If you want, we could test this out on your suit and we what we could come up with."

"Truly, we can test it out on the suit to see how it enhances its performance in combat."

Cobb walks toward Kenari with a blueprint for the Rapid-

Blade. Kenari takes a look at the blueprint, measuring the lines presented on the sheet to the detail of the new set of equipment.

"As you already know, this blueprint is an example of how we can enhance the Swordmobile."

"The Swordmobile?" Kenari gestured. "The phrases of the masses' rubbing off on you, Steven?"

"I wouldn't say that. But I think Swordmobile sounds more exciting than Rapid-Blade."

"We've come to call it the Rapid-Blade for a reason. We don't name things without the name itself having a purpose to the object."

"Truly, I will need the two of you to begin on these as soon as you can. I have a meeting with John Terror tonight concerning the whereabouts of this Sir Onyx man and the trails of Slade and Carr."

"John Terror, the Spiritual Assassin?" Steven asked. "He's here in Retropolis?"

"For the time being. We have a common enemy as of late."

"We'll get to work on these for you, Ken." Blake said. "It won't take us much time to complete."

"I'm well aware of your speedy process, Jacob."

Kenari exited the weapons room while Blake and Cobb went to work on the new improvements of the swordsuit and the Rapid-Blade.

Later in the day at the Clark Estate, Kenari sat with Allison inside the Swordlair. She sees him observing the swordsuit and the

Sword of the Elohim.

"So, you plan on meeting Terror tonight?"

"That is the plan, honey. We can work together in stopping Onyx and the other crime lords from doing their dirty work."

"What happens after the two of you stop them?"

"Terror returns to Chicago and I continue my work as usual."

"You could've called in other members of the Creed to assist you on this. I could've aided you."

"How could you aid me when your training is not complete. I don't want you going out on the field when you're not fully prepared."

"I know."

Kenari walked over to Allison and hugged her. They kissed one another before Kenari grabbed the swordsuit and his sword from the closet.

That night in an alleyway, Slade and Carr stood with new henchmen. They have commanded them to guard the alleyway by any means of force. Gazing at their watches, counting the time.

"Where is this Onyx fellow?" Slade said. "He told us to meet him here right at this spot."

"Don't fret yourself, Elliot." Carr said. "The man will be here."

The sounds of a car are heard approaching the alleyway. A black car, which stops directly at the end of the alley. Out of the back door walks out Sir Onyx, wearing a black suit with a red shirt and his known black mask. He walks toward Slade and Carr.

"I know I am late by a few seconds, but I am here in the flesh."

"About time. So, why are we meeting out here instead of a secure building." Slade said. "The Swordman could be out here."

"So, what."

"What do you mean so what? You've seen what he did to our men back at the warehouse."

"I did, and I thoroughly enjoyed the event."

"Son of a bitch." Carr said. "Enjoyed it."

"That's not why I called the two of you to meet me here. I called you both here to meet another man. A man that is well known in the crime underworld of Retropolis."

Slade and Carr spot another man walking down the alleyway with four guards around him. The man is of African American descent, wearing a dark blue suit with a dark blue trench coat over the suit. Slade looks at the man, thinking to himself.

"We've met before in the past, haven't we?"

"Yes, we have, Mr. Slade. It is an honor to also meet the well-known Ramon Lamono Carr."

"Pleasure's all mine. So, who are you?"

"Jacques Conley. But the criminal underworld knows me simply as J."

"So, why are we meeting you here with Onyx?" Slade said. "You both have some sort of idea that could enhanced our Utopia plan into full effect?"

"Yes, we surely do." J said.

One of J's guards approaches him with a black bag. J takes the bag and opens it. Slade and Carr question what he could be pulling out of the bag as they take several steps back. Onyx laughs at their fear.

"For two of the most feared crime lords in Retropolis, you both seem to be afraid."

From the black bag, J pulls out an object that appears to be made of ore with a golden color to it. Slade and Carr take steps forward to observe the object. Never seeing an object such as it before.

"What the hell is that supposed to be?" Carr said.

"I have a fetish with the art of mysticism. Where do you believe the name of the Fable Mountains comes from?"

"What is that thing supposed to do to help us?" Slade said. "We bash people in the heads with it?"

"No, Elliot. With this artifact, we can raise beings from the other realms to do the heavy work for us."

"Hold on a second, what beings and what realms are you talking about?"

"While the four of us deal with the Utopia Conspiracy, the beings that derive from this ancient object will take care of The Swordman for us. Get him out of our way permanently."

"You sure about this?"

"J has done his due diligence on this ancient artifact and knows more about its sources than the three of us combined." Onyx said. "Trust him on this matter as I have already hired a group of special mercenaries to deal with The Swordman until we find a place of refuge."

"I'm in." Carr said. "What about you, Slade?"

Slade turns to Carr and takes a look at Onyx and J before

nodding his head, accepting the agreement between them.

On the other side of Retropolis, Terror stands atop a building, overlooking the city. He heard metal clanking the building, hearing the sound of a cable being pulled. Behind him jumps The Swordman from the edge of the building. Terror grins, turning to face him.

"You do know how to sneak up on people. The ones without enhanced senses that is."

"Have you found any leads on Onyx or the other crime lords?"

"I have not. I have discovered that he must've sent The Party People back to Chicago because they're no longer able to be found in this city."

The Swordman nods. "That's a start."

While talking, the sound of a whip hits the building. They turn around, seeing a woman dressed in black leather standing. She removes her goggles and stares at them.

"I didn't expect to see you up here, Swordman. Who's the other guy?"

"What are you doing here, Huntswoman?"

"I'm here to see you of course. It's a good night to be out."

"This is The Huntswoman." Terror said. "The one that steals for a living and enjoys causing misery to others."

"That's me, honey."

"You didn't answer my question."

"I said I'm here to see you and I heard about your little search for that Sir Onyx guy."

"We're looking into it. We don't need your help, Catherine."

"Well, always throws me off to do some other form of work while you get to have all the fun."

"She calls this fun?" Terror asked.

"This isn't fun." The Swordman said. "It's war."

"A war that you can't possibly win on your own. That's why you're the leader of a Creed. They're meant to aid you in situations like this."

"The Creed have others across the earth. Handling their own territories. No need to bother them."

A gunshot blasts is heard as the bullet flying toward them. Deflected by The Swordman's forearm spikes down to the roof of the building. Terror stands his guard as he draws two handguns from his trench coat. Huntswoman twirls her whip made of titanium cable.

"The hell did that come from?" Terror said.

"It came from them."

They turn, seeing five individuals standing on the roof with them. The Swordman details at their uniforms, covered in black Kevlar armor with red and gray layering. The five are wearing militaristic masks, some cover their whole heads as others cover only a portion of their faces. They are set with an array of firearms at their disposal, all aimed at Swordman, Terror, and Huntswoman.

"I know those uniforms." The Swordman said. "I've dealt with them years past."

"Who are these guys?" Huntswoman asked.

"They call themselves The Exchange Force. A pair of

mercenaries for hire.”

“Sir Onyx paid us a lot of money to take you out, Swordman.” One of the mercenaries said. “That’s exactly what we’re here to do.”

The Swordman, Terror, and Huntswoman have a standoff with The Exchange Force. Weapons locked and loaded toward each other as Swordman slowly pulls out his sword and holds it against his chest and shoulder.

“Make the first move.” The Swordman stated.

III

THE EXCHANGE FORCE

The Exchange Force begin firing their firearms at Swordman, Terror, and Huntswoman. Terror is hit by the bullets, Huntswoman swiftly moves through the firing and Swordman deflects the bullets with his sword. Terror looks at his wounds and they heal within seconds.

"Always a keeper." Terror said with a grin.

He gets to his feet, running towards the Exchange Force as the bullets shoot through him. Feeling the pain from the gunfire, Terror continues to run, swiping his sword across one of their chests, cutting into their armor. He rams one of the Forcers, punches them in the face.

"Keep fighting them." The Swordman said. "They'll give up sooner than expected when they understand they can't take us down."

"Hope your right, Swords." said Huntswoman.

They continued to fight the Exchange Force across the rooftop. Swordman punches one of the Forcers in the face, grabs them by the neck and slams them onto the rooftop. He uses his sword to cut through the chest armor.

"They're almost finished."

Inside their secure base across Retropolis, Sir Onyx and J, oversee a table where the ancient artifact has been placed. The doors open, entering Slade and Carr with their bodyguards.

"Glad you could make it, boys." Onyx said. "Thought you wouldn't be able to attend this little special occasion of ours."

"We're here and we're ready for our plan to come into fruition." Carr said. "So, tell us when does it all start?"

"It begins at this very moment." J said. "Are you ready for it to begin?"

J walks over to the table, he grabs the artifact, raises it up above his head. He begins to speak in Latin toward the artifact, as if it can hear him and understand the language. A bluish hue starts to form out of the artifact. Slade and Carr slowly, but surely take steps back in fear with Onyx overlooking J and the artifact.

"Beautiful." Onyx said.

J held the artifact tightly before placing it back onto the table. From the artifact fires a beam of light, which traveled through the middle of the base, creating a portal.

"The hell is that?!" Slade said. Pointing at the portal.

"Some damn hole!" Carr replied. "I don't know what to make of it."

Strange and obscure sounds rumble from the portal. J approaches and stares into the portal with a smile on his face. His curiosity has set in. Onyx rubs his hands together. Savoring the moment. Slade and Carr lean against the wall as the sounds increase, moving closer toward the portal.

"Here they come." J said.

The portal flashes several times and through the quick flashes of light appear three beasts. J stood before them still, with his arms spread out as fear consumes both Slade and Carr. Onyx becomes hesitant, not making any movements as he witnesses the three beasts. The beasts enter the base from the portal. After the move from the portal, it closes. J approaches the beasts without fear.

"Gentlemen, these are our weapons of the utopia."

Slade stares at the beasts. Seeing things, he's never come across. He glances at one. It references something he's known about before. Pointing at the beast.

"Is that a sasquatch?" Slade said.

"Yes, it is." said. J. "Though, it prefers to call itself The Bigfoot."

"The Bigfoot, eh?" said Carr. "Sure. Why not."

"What's that other one?" Slade said. "The bird/human hybrid? Some kind of griffin creature?"

"It's called the Bird-Thing, Elliot." Onyx said. "Appears to be a known legend in history."

"Ain't this last one?" Carr questioned. "Looks like a werewolf to me."

The Werewolf turns around. staring into Carr's eyes, it glares intensely. Carr leans against the wall as the Werewolf walks toward him, very slowly. Slade moves over as does Onyx. J stands by the table watching. Carr backs up against the wall as the Werewolf leans in toward his face. Sniffing.

"I don't need an introduction." The Werewolf said. "I am what I appear to be. But, there is a catch unto me."

"You're immortal." said J. "I've heard the legends of an immortal werewolf that was once the assistant of a dark god. Fascinating lore to be told."

"It is no legend nor folklore. It is true, and that particular dark god will be making his return very soon."

The Immortal Werewolf as it's called, approaches J. Towering over him. J has no other option but to look up at the Werewolf.

"Why did you call us out and why are we here?"

"We require your assistance in taking this city."

"What city?"

"The city of Retropolis."

The Werewolf moves toward a window, looking outside. He sees the skyline view of Retropolis. The Werewolf turns back to J and glares at the Bigfoot and the Bird-Thing.

"Be that as it may, we will do what we must for you to succeed. We'll tear this city apart by every inch of its structures."

"You must beware of The Swordman." Slade said. "You must."

"In my time, I've dealt with many swordsmen and all have fallen. Another one won't be a problem."

"But, this one is different." J mentioned. "He carries the Sword of the Elohim in his possession."

The Werewolf stops, looking over to J with tension in his eyes. The words are familiar to him.

"The Sword of the Elohim."

"Yes."

"Then, this is no ordinary swordsmen. This is one of them Swordmen from their Creed. Let me deal with him."

The Werewolf signals Bigfoot and the Bird-Thing out of the base and toward the city. Slade and Carr run to J with concern as Onyx looks outside, watching the three beasts move toward Downtown Retropolis.

"Are you sure we can trust those monsters?" Slade said.

"I think we can, Elliot." Carr said with a little tremble in his voice. "I mean, you saw them didn't you. Their stature and presence."

"They will do their part and after all is clear, we'll have this city under our control and our utopia will begin."

The three beasts enter the downtown area of Retropolis. The Werewolf signaled Bigfoot to move east and the Bird-Thing west as he chose to deal with the northern and southern regions of Retropolis. The beasts began to terrorize and destroy all that is in their sight. Civilians ran amok in the city to avoid being attacked or killed. The Bigfoot rams through the streets, tackling vehicles. The Bigfoot bursts through a store, grabbing the clerk and throwing them through a window. On the western side of downtown, the Bird-Thing attacks civilians and throws them across the streets, some landing through windows of nearby buildings.

"Must destroy all." The Bird-Thing said. "All must be destroyed."

The Retropolis Police Department phone line is ringing constantly of civilians calling to tell them about the beasts attacking the city. Many of the officers decline the call, stating its nothing more than an average prank call. One civilian ran into the department covered in blood and a scratch mark on their chest.

"Help us." the civilians said before falling to the ground

Commissioner Austin walks out of his office to check on the civilians but realizes they're dead. Justine and Cash approach him from behind and stare down at the deceased civilian.

"What should we do, Commissioner?" said Justine.

"We're going out there to help them." Austin said. "Those phone calls weren't damn prank calls, you idiots!"

Austin grabs his coat and leaves the department with Justine and Cash following along with other few officers. As they drive away from the department toward downtown. Austin grabs his walkie.

"Justine, when we reach downtown, make sure you have your firearm ready."

"Understood."

The Swordman, Terror, and Huntswoman continue battling it out with the Exchange Force on the rooftop. The Force has slowed down with The Swordman easily being able to take them down with a couple of attacks. While they continue to fight, they hear the sirens of the police cars. One of the Forcers looked down at the street, seeing the police lights blinking.

"We have police approaching, team!"

The Exchange Force leaves the rooftop while Swordman and Terror watch. Huntswoman tries to catch one of them but fails in the process.

"Shit. I could've had him."

She looks onward, seeing the police lights coming near the building. She turns around toward Swordman and Terror, preparing to flee the scene.

"Where are you going, Huntswoman?" Terror said.

"I'm leaving this area. The damn cops are coming."

"They're not coming for us." The Swordman said.

"What makes you say that?"

He points toward downtown, seeing the smoke and fire rising from the ground into the sky. They heard the screams coming from the sight.

"Something's going on downtown. We have to check it out."

"Leave that to the damn cops." Terror said. "We need to follow the tracks of those Forcers."

"We can do that another time. Something bigger is taking place and I would like to find out what it is."

From the police car, Justine sees people standing on the rooftop. She gets Cash's attention and he looks.

"Maybe those are just some kids playing around, Justine."

"They're too old to be children. We're going to see who they are."

She drives over to the building to see who they are as The Swordman jumps down from the rooftop to the ground, Huntswoman follows him with Terror coming last. They look around after finding themselves in an alleyway. Terror approaches his motorcycle before looking around and not seeing another vehicle in sight. He looks to The Swordman and Huntswoman.

"Any of you got a ride?" Terror said.

"I have a ride." said The Swordman.

He presses a button on his wrist gauntlet and the sound of a boom comes from the sky and from the sky emerges an aircraft. Shaped as a sword in great detail. Its name is the Sky-Rapier or what the civilians would call the Swordwing. He raises his arm up, preparing to grapple onto the craft. Huntswoman latches onto him.

"I'm riding alongside with you."

"Fair enough."

He fires his grappling hook onto the craft. They reach the cockpit and enter. Terror looks up at the craft and in front of the alley appear the police. The car stopped, and Justine exits, with her gun drawn on Terror. Cash gets out of the car and does the same. Only with a cheeky smile.

"Freeze! Get off the bike and stand against the wall!"

"Really, lady." Terror said with a smirk.

"I said get off the damn bike!"

"You poor women of today. Seeking power and authority in places where you don't need it."

Justine looks up, hearing the engine and seeing the Sky-Rapier.

"The hell is that thing?!"

"Looks like some sort of flying sword if you ask me." said Cash. "Even has a hilt."

The bike engine roars with Terror speeding past them. Going

down the street, heading downtown while the Sky-Rapier flies off from the area.

"Damn it." Justine said."

Justine and Cash get into the car, proceeding to follow them. Speeding down the street, Cash looks and see Terror in front of them.

"I've never seen someone wear that type of clothing around here."

"Because, he's not from around here."

"How would you know that, Detective?"

"Because he's John Terror. A wanted man. A murderer and an assassin."

"You've done your homework."

"You should have done yours."

Almost near downtown, The Swordman flies the Sky-Rapier with Huntswoman sitting in the passenger's seat. She looks around at the interior of the craft. Relaxing herself somewhat.

"You never told me you had a craft of your own."

"It's not my own. It belongs to the Order."

"Oh. Do tell me about it."

"You already know enough about the Creed. You were invited to join, but you turned down the offer. Remember?"

"Because I like the value of being a loner in a big city."

"Suit yourself. We're coming up on downtown. Prepare yourself."

He lands the Sky-Rapier atop a building. He and

Huntswoman exit, jumping down from the building to the ground. Terror catches them in his sight, riding over toward them. Stopping his bike.

"I see the police are on your trail." Huntswoman said.

"They'll soon be on yours."

The Swordman looked at downtown, seeing how the civilians are running from three different locations of the city.

"So, what's your game plan in this, Swords?" Terror said.

"It appears that we'll have to split up on this one. Terror, you take the western division. Huntswoman, take the eastern section, and I'll deal with the center piece."

"Fair enough for me." Huntswoman said as she left.

Terror looks at The Swordman.

"What are we supposed to do about Onyx and J?"

"They're involved in all of this. I can assure you of that."

Terror nods before heading into downtown. The Swordman walks into the downtown area of Retropolis, seeing Huntswoman and Terror entering the western and eastern sections. He stands center of Retropolis with his sword out and against his chest.

"Where are you?"

Huntswoman runs through the eastern division, aiding the remaining civilians to escape as the area is covered with debris and flames. While aiding the civilians, she hears a deep, graveling roar coming from behind her. She turned around to see the Bigfoot standing behind her. Unaware of her surroundings, she stood still. Lost for words.

"A bigfoot did this?" She said with confusion. "A bigfoot?!"

The Bigfoot runs toward her as she flips over it and dropkick it in the back. The Bigfoot turned around and swiped her into a turned over car. She smirked.

"This is new." She said humorously.

In the western section, as Terror aids the civilians and helps them leave, he hears wings above him and as he glances up, the Bird-Thing grabs him by the shoulders with its claws and drops him onto the ground. Terror looks up and sees the Bird-Thing as it lands in front of him and screams toward him.

"The hell are you supposed to be?" Terror said. "Some sort of man-bird?"

The Bird-Thing flies toward him and Terror begins firing his guns at the Bird-Thing. Catching a few shots into its wings, the Bird-Thing swipes Terror in the head with its wing and uses its flight to ram Terror through a window of a shopping center.

"Son of a bitch."

The Swordman stood still in the center section of downtown Retropolis. Listening closely, he caught the sound of something coming toward his location in the distance. He doesn't make a move, only stares at what's in front of him and he sees it. The Immortal Werewolf walking toward him holding the head of a dead body in his hand. The Werewolf stopped and stared.

"You are him."

"Who am I exactly?"

"You are the one Death spoke about ages ago. The one who would be her adversary until time's end. You are The Swordman."

"I am and who are you?"

"I am the Immortal Werewolf. My master gave me the name Dyclos."

"Who would your master be exactly?"

"You'll know when he wants to make himself known to this modern era."

"So, why are you here? Following your master's orders?"

"My master didn't give me this particular mission. However, a man who called himself, J, needed my assistance and I gave it to him."

"So, J conjured you from your dimensional home and brought you here."

"He did. I and the other entities that he requires for aid have been brought here."

"I'm going to give you ten seconds to communicate with those other beings and leave this place."

"What if I don't do what you've told me?"

"I'll have to kill you."

"You didn't hear what I said. I am immortal. No mortal weapon could penetrate my hide nor injure me."

The Swordman raises up his sword, pointing it at the Werewolf.

"This is no mortal weapon."

"I know about that sword. I've seen many wield it in my time. It's been passed down to you. Do you know how many Swordmen

I've killed over the ages? How many have felt my teeth sink into their flesh and drink their blood?"

"I am aware of those you have killed. The reality is I'm not one of them. I am The Swordman."

The Werewolf lunges toward Swordman and he swipes the beast with his sword, cutting through its hairy flesh. The Werewolf stops for a moment, glancing at the wound on his shoulder. He looks at The Swordman, who's standing still and ready for the fight.

"I am impressed." The Werewolf said. "Appears you are not like the others from before."

"Enough talk." said The Swordman.

"Enough talk indeed."

The two clashed with each other. By the sword and claws.

The Retropolis Police enter the downtown area, Commissioner Austin split the officers in pairs, sending them off in different directions. While walking through and seeing the surviving civilians, he heard clashing coming from in front of him. He decides to run over to the site to see what is making the sound and when he inches closer, he sees The Swordman and the Immortal Werewolf fighting each other.

"Is that The Swordman?" Austin said.

Justine runs up behind Austin, seeing Swordman and Werewolf battling it out. She reaches for her gun, but Austin halts her.

"Don't."

"Why not? We have them where we want them, Commissioner."

"Not yet, Detective. Hold on a bit."

In the western division, Terror continues to battle the Bird-Thing as it continuously swoops up in the air, ramming Terror into the buildings nearby. Terror lays on the ground, taking a breather for a second. He stands up.

"Where do these things come from?" He said.

Waiting for the Bird-Thing to swoop past him again. He waits and waits until he hears the screeching in the air. He looked up and sees the Bird-Thing coming near him.

"Here we go." Terror said.

The Bird-Thing swooped toward Terror, he jumped above it and latches onto its neck. Bird-Thing screeches as it tries to knock Terror off its back. Terror holds on and pulls out a dagger and begins stabbing the flying monster in its back. From the amount of pain, Bird-Thing crashes down into a section of fire.

In the eastern section, Huntswoman finally managed to take down the Bigfoot and held him against a set of blocks which sat in the open space. Using her whip to hold the Bigfoot's neck as she pulled it into the block section, trapping the beast in between. Police officers caught her as she ran from the scene. While chasing her, the officers paused and stopped. Staring at the Bigfoot.

"Is that a sasquatch?" An officer said.

"Tall, hairy, and smelly? Yeah, it's one of them things."

The officers arrived at the scene in the western region, seeing Bird-Thing laying in the fire. They raise their guns up as Terror walks through the flames, skinned burned and his clothing ripped. Damped with blood from himself and the Bird-Thing.

"Freeze!"

"Officers. Are you sure this is what you want? If you please, move out of my way and you will not be harmed."

The officers stand still as Terror walks past them, grabbing his trench coat from the ground, walking away from the site. The officers watch him walk away.

"Did we just let him go?"

"Keep quiet or he'll gut us up."

The Swordman and Immortal Werewolf continue to battle as Swordman takes his sword and swipes the abdomen of the Werewolf. He fell to one knee as Swordman stood over him.

"What are you waiting for?" The Werewolf asked. "Finish me."

"Don't rush your death."

The Swordman rose up his sword. Set over the Werewolf's neck, prepared for decapitation. Justine runs past Austin toward The Swordman.

"Justine!" Austin yelled.

The Swordman turned his attention, Justine ran toward him.

He kept his sword held over the Werewolf's neck. Motionless.

"Put the sword down!" Justine commanded, aiming her gun at The Swordman.

"If I don't, what will you do?"

"Don't tempt me, vigilante!"

Justine held her gun on him as he turned and swiped his sword toward her. She stumbled for a quick second. Thoughts may have changed. Maybe.

"What's wrong, Detective? Scared?"

"I'm placing you under arrest for your act of vigilantism."

"There's no time for this nonsense."

The Swordman turned back to the Werewolf, but the Werewolf was gone. Typically vanished out of the air. He looks back at Justine and sees Austin standing in the distance.

"Another time for this little meeting."

The Sky-Rapier flies over them in haste. The Swordman grapples onto the flying craft, leaving the area.

Austin approaches Justine with somewhat of an anger. She places her gun back into its holster.

"I told you to wait for instructions."

"I know. But we had him in our sights and I did not want to let that slip."

"He did say another time."

In the craft, Swordman watched on a map, the tracing of the mystical energy around the Werewolf. The map led him to a small warehouse not far out of Retropolis grounds. He turned the craft, heading toward the site.

Onyx looked out of the window at the base, seeing the Sky-Rapier in the air coming towards them. Slade and Carr can also see the craft approaching. They decide to make a run for it, to leave the base. Onyx turns to J with some concern in his voice.

"The Swordman is heading this way in some sort of craft! What are we supposed to do?"

J, standing by the artifact sitting on the table, takes off his coat, laying it on the table, raises up a sword of his own. He moves, standing in the middle of the room.

"Let him come and we'll end this ourselves."

IV

<u>CONSPIRACY IS TRUTH</u>

The Sky-Rapier landed quietly in a field in front of the base. Seeing the craft on the ground, Onyx moved with slow, but hasty steps back from the door. J stood in the middle of the room with his sword in hand.

"What are you going to do, J?" Onyx wondered.

"I'm going to take out The Swordman. After that, we can get back to our business."

They wait patiently for The Swordman to enter the base. Within several seconds, the doors burst open as The Swordman stands there, staring down J and Onyx. J smiles.

"Finally, you've come to see us."

"The word appears to be truth." The Swordman said. "J and Sir Onyx working together as one."

"You have to work with others for business ventures in order to grow stronger and bigger." J said. "You and your Creed must understand the form of business."

"We do. Not under illegal purposes."

The Swordman sees Onyx standing by the backdoor. Shaking and hesitant to take another step inside the room. Swordman later looks over at the table, seeing the artifact and its glow.

"That device is what released those creatures in the city."

"It surely is." J said. "I take it you've dealt with them or at least one of them."

"The Werewolf. It disappeared before I was able to finish it off. I suspected you called them back to this place for healing."

"I didn't call back any of them. They're free to roam around as they please. They've been around much longer than I. Plus, they know more about this planet than the three of us in this room."

The Swordman raises up his sword.

"Oh no." Onyx said. "Damn it no!"

"It's time we finish this event, J."

"I agree."

J runs toward Swordman, swiping the sword in the air, Swordman dodges the swipes. He clashes his sword against J's. Onyx attempts to escape the base, but finds the backdoor jammed shut, possibly by Slade and Carr's early escape.

"This damn door won't open!"

The Swordman and J continue to have a sword duel with the two clashing their swords together along with several physical attacks toward one another. Swordman clashes the sword, hitting J in the face with his elbow, later flipping him over onto the ground. J kicks up back to his feet, kicking Swordman in the abdomen and rams him into the wall with a spear. J delivers several jabs to Swordman's ribs and head butts him. J goes to uppercut Swordman, but he catches J's arm, ramming his forearm into J's face and slams him through one of the wooden tables. Onyx decides to watch the fight between the two, uncertain of what he should do.

"Holy shit." Onyx said.

The Swordman kicks J in the face and knocks him onto the floor. J looks around and finds himself on the ground with Swordman's sword nearly against his throat.

"I suggest you cease yourself from certain death." The Swordman said. "Unless you want to see The Father today and now."

Onyx grabs a chair that was leaning against the wall. He runs toward The Swordman, preparing to hit him with it. Swordman turns around and takes the chair from Onyx. He raises the chair and hits him in the head with it, cracking the skull mask from the impact. Onyx falls to the ground, unconscious. J tries to trip Swordman, but ultimately fails when Swordman takes his sword and stabs the tip of it into J's calf.

"Shit!" J yelled.

"Now you'll stop."

The Swordman hears the police sirens approaching and leaves the base. He takes another look at the table and realizing the artifact is gone.

"What the hell."

Hearing the officers outside, he leaves the base. Austin, Justine, Cash, and a few other officers enter the building. They look around, seeing the destroyed table. They look to the floor, seeing Onyx knocked out and J grunting in pain from the stab wound. Holding his leg.

"You think he was here, Commissioner?" Justine said.

"I certainly believe so."

"Of course, The Swordman was here!" J said. "He stabbed me in my leg and knocked out Onyx over there!"

"Shut your mouth, Conley." Austin said. "We don't need to hear another word from you."

Near the brink of dawn, Swordman finds Terror on his motorcycle near the highway. Terror stops his bike on the side of the highway as The Swordman approaches him in the rapid-blade. Swordman exits the vehicle.

"Appears you're returning to Chicago."

"I am. Seems the mission is over."

"It would seem to be the case as of now."

"Any whereabouts on Sir Onyx or J?"

"They've been placed in Rockward Penitentiary for a period. No word on their release dates."

Terror nodded with a grin.

"That's fair enough. I didn't see Huntswoman after I left downtown."

"She returned to her home more than likely. She'll pop up again soon enough."

Terror gets onto his motorcycle and starts it up as The Swordman enters the rapid-blade.

"Take care of yourself now." The Swordman said.

"I will as always."

Terror rides off onto the highway leaving Canada. The Rapid-

Blade does a U-turn and drives off as the sun begins to set over the horizon.

Later during the day, Kenari goes down to the Swordlair to do some studying on what's taking place around the world and in Retropolis. Upon entering the lair, he spots a man sitting down at his desk. Kenari prepares himself for the possible fight as he cautiously makes his way into the lair.

"Who in the hell are you and who let you in here?"

"No one let me in here, Kenari Clark." The man said. "I let myself in."

"Explain who you are and why are you here?"

The man stands up, wearing mostly all black with some white and silver lining in his Kevlar clothing. He looks militaristic. Almost like a General. Kenari reads his body language. He knows he works in some operation that deals with global situations.

"I'm Evan Nader. Colonel Evan Nader of T.I.T.A.N."

"I'm aware of the agency. What's that have to do with you inside my lair?"

Nader turns around, glancing at the swordsuit sitting in the closet.

"There's something coming that will need your full attention."

"What kind of something?"

"I'm sure you're doing your studying as to where the artifact went during your fight with J."

"How do you know about that?"

"I have eyes and ears everywhere, Mr. Clark. Nothing can

possibly escape my senses."

"What about the artifact do you know?"

"The artifact concerns not only Retropolis. But the entire planet and could in fact effect the universe entirely."

"Do you know where it could be?"

"My team is currently tracking it down as we speak."

Kenari takes a seat. Nader grabs the chair and sits in front of him, waiting for him to speak.

"Tell me what this is and how I can be of help."

Nader smiles.

"Very well."

CHOSEN SON
GODS AND TITANS

I

BARGAINED ARRANGEMENT

The beam of light shot down from the sky into the KexInc. Building. Kex Kendrick takes a look up as the beam surrounds him and pulls him in, vanishing into the air with Kex along with it. Kex finds himself flowing through the air, upwards into the beam of light, he seems to savor the moment, having a sense of fear creeping into his consciousness. In a flash, the beam of light vanishes with Kex finding himself in a room that looks similar to a council room.

"What is this place?" Kex asked himself. "Where am I?"

Kex turned around, finding himself standing in the presence of the Twelve Olympians. He glanced around, coming to the realization he was transported from his office to Mount Olympus. Standing in the middle of their council. He gazed in awe at the Twelve Olympians and their stature.

They are: Dionysus, the god of wine, celebrations, and ecstasy. Hestia, the goddess of hearth and of the right ordering of the domestically and family. Hermes, the messenger of the gods and the god of commerce, thieves, eloquence, and streets. Aphrodite, the goddess of love, beauty, and desire. Ares, the god of war, violence, and bloodshed. Artemis, the goddess of hunting, virginity, archery, the moon, and animals. Apollo, the god of light and prophecy.

Athena, the goddess of wisdom, reason, science, defense and strategic warfare. Demeter, the goddess of fertility, agriculture, nature, and seasons. Poseidon, the god of the sea, earthquakes, and tidal waves. Hera, the Queen of the gods and the goddess of marriage. Lastly is Zeus, the King of the gods and the god of the sky, lightning, thunder, law, order, and justice. He is the ruler of Mount Olympus and the one responsible for bringing Kex to Mount Olympus.

One Olympian is missing, which would've been the thirteen is Hephaestus, the master blacksmith and craftsman of the gods, also the god of fire and forgery.

Zeus stares at Kex, noticing his trembling at the presence of the Greek gods. He holds his hand up toward him.

"Don't be afraid, Kex Kendrick." Zeus said. "You are here on urgent matters."

"I could've guessed that. What matters are urgent enough to bring me here without a warning?"

"Taltus."

"I do not know who you speak of."

Zeus waves his hands into the air. In front of Kex forms a small portal, looking like a mirror. The portal gives Kex the ability to see nearly everything on the earth. The portal twists and warps. As if it's moving a quick speed. It stops warping once it reaches Enigma City, where Kex sees The Powerman fighting the Dragon Gargoyle. Kex's mouth drops slightly.

"You speak of him."

"I do. I know more about him than any mortal on the face of the earth. He came from this realm. I banished him to the earth. To live amongst the humans. Not for humility, but for the fact that he is not one of us. He is a hybrid being. A mixture of both titan and god. I do not allow such treachery to take place atop my mountain."

"What do you need me to do, King of the gods?"

"I already have something prepared for you to begin with. I know of your conversations with some extraterrestrial entity and I understand that he is in agreement with our terms. He appears to be an intelligent being."

"He is. He is slowly making his way toward earth. It will take almost a few months before his arrival."

"He can take his time. For right now, I will send a series of tests to earth for Taltus to handle. To see where he himself fits between gods and titans."

"I am all for your tests and I will do what I can to aid you in this predicament."

"Kex Kendrick, remember this. When we rid this universe of Taltus, there are still others like him who live among your kind on earth. This will send a message to them and after they receive it, will kill them as well."

"I couldn't agree with you more."

Zeus raises his arm, summoning the beam of light. The beam reappears over Kex. He stares at it, hovering above his head. Kex looks over to Zeus.

"I am sending you back to your realm, Kex Kendrick. Remember what I have spoken this day. The tests will begin once you return to your world and you will see that our plan is in full effect."

"I understand."

Zeus set down his arm, commanding the beam of light to swallow Kex, returning him to his office. Within seconds, Kex was back in the office. He looks outside the windows, realizing an entire day had passed on earth, whereas his visit to Mount Olympus felt like minutes. Beatrice Mercer enters through the door, seeing Kex beginning to sit down.

"Sir, where have you been? We couldn't find you at all

yesterday."

"I was on an important business meeting. I'm here now and everything is alright."

"I was only checking up on you, sir."

"I understand your loyalty toward me, and I respect it highly. It shows your determination to be by my side."

"Yes sir."

Beatrice exits Kex's office. He continues staring outside the window, overlooking Enigma City.

"The tests are about to unfold on you, Taltus. Let's see what you're truly made of."

On the outskirts of Enigma City, Stephanie Vale drives down the highway, searching for the proposed sight of The Powerman's Fortress of Cytron. Alex sits in the passenger seat. He looks out through the window.

"You sure they said he lives out here?"

"That's what has been mentioned for over a period of time. Said he lives out in the middle of nowhere, surrounded by ice."

Alex nods, looking outside again, seeing only grass and dirt around them.

"You sure you know where you're going? Because I only see grass out here. Dirt too. There are even crops growing out here. Looked like a cornfield back there. You think it was a cornfield or just some field?"

"I know where I'm going, Alex. So, stay quiet."

"I'm only asking."

"I said stay quiet."

"You sure you want me to stay quiet?"

"Yes. Shut up please."

Alex nods quickly. He sits back in the seat.

"Ok. I'm not talking during the entire ride out here and

back."

"Whatever you say."

She continues her search, during the same time, at the fortress itself, The Powerman sits inside his throne room. Meditating and in perfect silence. His personal melody of choosing. His eyes are closed. Using his heightened senses, he hears his surroundings close and afar off. He listens in closely, beginning to hear a flapping sound flowing through the air. Not close to the fortress, but afar off. He could sense where the flapping was coming from and what direction it was headed. The sound was of large wings, flowing through the sky. After several seconds, his eyes open, glowing gold.

"He's here. Again."

He stands up, exiting the fortress. He flies into the air, following the one responsible for the winged sounds.

II

TEST OF COMBATANTS

The Powerman flew through the sky, breaking the sound barrier as he went along. Coming up on the winged sound he heard back at the fortress. Flying over the wilderness, he looked forward, seeing the entity responsible for the winged sounds.

"I see he's brought you back." Powerman said.

The Powerman flew faster to reach as the entity turns around, revealing itself to be the Dragon Gargoyle. The Gargoyle lunges itself toward Powerman, tackling him down into an open field. Powerman rolls on the ground. The Gargoyle lands near him.

"Your trials have begun, Taltus."

"What trials?"

"The ones standing in front of you. A test if you will. By the King of the gods."

"Zeus huh."

"Are you ready, titagod?!"

"I am. I'm going to beat you down again. This time worse than before and there's not a single innocent person around to hold my power back"

Powerman swoops over to the Dragon Gargoyle, picking him up and slamming him around the field. Throwing him toward a set of trees, thereby entering the woods. Powerman kicks and slaps the broken trees out of his way, seeing Dragon Gargoyle on the ground, covered in branches.

"Had enough?" Powerman said.

"Don't try to get smart with me."

"It was only a question."

The Dragon Gargoyle tries to attack The Powerman with several blows to the chest. Powerman grabs both his fists and headbutts the Gargoyle.

Falling to the ground, Powerman holds him by his throat, hovering in the air. His dark blue cape flowing through the wind. His eyes set on Gargoyle's eyes.

"I'm ending this first trial now."

"You think I'm easy?! Wait till you see what he has in store for you. For all your kind!"

"I am the only one of my kind. There is no others."

The Powerman's eyes turn a shining gold. Through them, releases the lightning vision, striking Gargoyle's face, burning him and electrocuting him. Gargoyle screams, shaking from the enduring pain. He falls out due to the attack, Powerman lays him on the ground and flies off.

"I'm going to find out what these trials are."

After several attempts to find the fortress, Stephanie turned the car around, returning to Enigma City. Alex shakes his head, Stephanie glares at him. Seeing him smiling.

"What's so funny?"

"I told you there's no ice out here. He must live up there near the North Pole or something."

"That wouldn't explain how he moves around so fast. He has to reside somewhere close to Enigma City. That is the only explanation that could have him coming into the city and leaving."

"You're underestimating his abilities, Stephanie. Look at the guy. He's something we've never seen in our lives. He has incredible strength and speed. Plus, he can fly and not with some armor suit or a gilding cape to do it. It's in his DNA. He is basically a god amongst men."

"I get your points, Alex. I do. But, that doesn't automatically explain how he could live so far away and appear here in minutes. Or in seconds. It doesn't add up."

Alex looks down at his phone, scrolling through the internet. He spots Kendrick's name. He turns at Stephanie, showing her the image of Kex on the internet. Stephanie shrugs.

"What does he have to do with anything that we talked about?"

"Think about it. A man such as Kex Kendrick has money and power to know things ordinary citizens don't know. He could know the location of Powerman's fortress."

"I doubt that, Alex."

"Just hear me out. Let's take a trip over to the Kendrick Corporations buildings and ask the man ourselves. See what he says. They say he's a nice guy to talk to."

"Where did you read that at? Social media?"

"Yeah. Can't go wrong there."

Stephanie shakes her head, continuing driving down the highway to Enigma City.

The Powerman hovered above the grounds. While in the air, he slightly caught the sound of a loud tremor of thunder above him. He looked up, gazing through the clouds. Standing within the cloud is Zeus himself. Glaring toward Taltus with anger.

"You've shown your face."

"You have passed the first test that I have given you, Taltus. Let's see if you can pass this next test."

"What test?"

From the distance, Powerman can hear the sounds of civilians screaming in Enigma City. Flying faster to reach the city, Zeus laughs at him, disappearing in the clouds. The Powerman flies faster, moving at mach speed in the air, zapping through the clouds like a thunderbolt.

"What have you done, Zeus?" The Powerman said. "What have you done."

He arrives at the small town, which is called Oval Town, a small-town that does business with Enigma City. In the town, The Powerman sees the civilians running for their lives. Terrified of something, in which Powerman proceeds to look. Seeing a large object in the distance. He hovers his way toward it, stopping immediately, staring at the object.

"What are you?"

The Powerman finds himself staring at a large gorilla, which stood almost over seven feet tall, covered in brownish black hair. The gorilla was destroying cars and hammering small buildings. The gorilla turns, seeing Powerman hovering from him in the distance. The gorilla roars at Powerman.

"Who are you if you can speak?" The Powerman said. "If not, make a gesture to my response."

The gorilla roars again, afterwards grin at Powerman. The gorilla drops the pieces of cars that were in its hand and only glares toward Powerman with its red eyes.

"I am your second test, Taltus." The gorilla said.

"You can speak?"

"I can speak because of Zeus. He pulled him from the jungles and gave me power beyond what I could've known. He also gave me the ability of speech. You may call me, Colosso."

"Very well. Colosso, I do not tend to harm you unless you leave this town immediately and return to Zeus or your jungle land."

"I will not leave this place until you are beneath my feet and your flesh is in my mouth."

"You asked for this, Colosso. I'm sorry for what is about to take place."

"As am I."

Colosso beams its own lightning vision from its own eyes toward Powerman, slamming him on the pavement. Powerman looks up toward Colosso, rubbing his chest from the blast.

"He has my abilities."

"I can also do this!"

Colosso blasts red radiation beams from his eyes, shoving Powerman back into the pavement, which knocks him into the window of a small diner. Colosso approaches the diner with Powerman slowly standing up. Surrounded by destroyed tables and broken glass.

"I thought you were some sort of titagod. That's what Zeus told me you were. A hybrid of titan and god. Doesn't appear that way to me."

"Because you haven't known what I can truly do."

The Powerman stands up and punches Colosso, he kicks him across the road, away from the diner. Colosso laugh, brushing off the pain from the kick. Seeing Powerman walking toward him.

"I want to do what the Gargoyle couldn't do and that's kill you where you stand!"

"Try it and see what happens of yourself."

The Powerman and Colosso collide into each other in the middle of Oval Town. Throwing punches and blows at one another, Colosso grabs Powerman, headbutts him, knocking him across the town. Colosso runs over and stomps onto Powerman. Colosso believes himself to win, he didn't expect Powerman to grab a hold of his leg and slam him into the road to where Powerman hovers above him and collapses onto his back with his boots. Colosso roars in pain.

"Give up, Colosso. To spare your own life."

"I will complete what Zeus has made me for. To kill you and

the titagods.”

“Again. There is no others. I am the only one.”

The Powerman pulls back his fist and rams Colosso in the head with such strength that it nearly breaks Colosso’s neck. Colosso falls to the ground and the sky thunders. Zeus appears again, this time in front of Powerman.

“You have taken out my second test. Interesting. You are proving yourself, Taltus. Something I dared you wouldn’t have achieved.”

“Is this nonsense over or do I have to take out more of your mindless soldiers?”

“There is one more. One more. But first, I demand you speak with Kex Kendrick of the matter.”

“Kex Kendrick? What does he have to do with this and what does he have to do with you?”

“We have an agreement with one another. To take you out.”

“Why don’t you take me out now if you can.”

Zeus laughed. Humoring the Powerman.

“It is not the time nor the place for such a battle. A battle which would be your last.”

“I will stop you.”

“Go see Kex Kendrick. Get all your answers from him. Trust me for one, he has them.”

Zeus disappears, taking Colosso with him. The Powerman nods his head, flying to Enigma City to confront Kex Kendrick.

III

CONFRONTING YOUR NEMESIS

Stephanie and Alex enter Enigma City, driving towards the KexInc. Building. Alex looks at the building and the amount of windows it has. Impressed.

"You think they need all those windows?"

"I wouldn't know, Alex."

"Because what if one cracks right, and someone is standing by one and it breaks apart and the person falls out of the window. Have they ever thought about that?"

"I'm sure they have, Alex. You could ask them once we get in."

"Oh, I will."

Stephanie inches her way toward the building, they spot The Powerman flying above them, going straight to the building as well. Alex shouts with excitement, frightening Stephanie.

"The hell was that for?!" Stephanie yelled. "Trying to cause a wreck?!"

"Did you see that?! It was him!"

"I know it was him and he's going to the building."

"Maybe to confront Kex Kendrick about his fortress. See, I told you the man knows something we don't."

Stephanie floors the gas pedal, driving faster to reach the building.

The Powerman flew toward the windows, searching them. He gazed upwards, catching Kex near the top of the building. He flew up the window, keeping his sights on Kex sitting at his desk. Within the office, Beatrice entered, like a bolt of lightning, Beatrice stared at the window, seeing The Powerman hovering behind Kex. She stopped and froze in place. Staring without words. Kex looked up from the desk to Beatrice. Noticing her frozen state.

"Beatrice, what is it?"

"He's behind you, sir."

Kex turned to the window. Finding himself face to face with The Powerman. A grin grew on his face as Taltus only stared and the stare wasn't a pleasant one. Kex opens the window, allowing Powerman inside the office. The two stare at each other with Beatrice lost for words and lost for actions.

"Boss...." Beatrice said.

"Leave us, Beatrice." Kex said. "I will be just fine. I've been waiting for this moment ever since he first showed up."

Beatrice leaves the office. Kex grins, staring at The Powerman.

"Finally." Kex said. "We meet."

"Seems like you've wanted to meet me for a while now."

"Oh, I have Powerman. I've wanted to meet you since the day you showed up in my city."

"Your city?"

"Precisely. This is my city. You trespassed onto what is mine. The people look at it today as if it's yours. Yours?! Yu weren't even born in this city. Let alone raised in it."

"I was raided by people who avoided the city at all costs. The noise and trouble the city life could bring was worse than living out in the middle of nowhere."

Kex sighs.

"You outskirt people. I take it you were raised by an agricultural family. An earthly one that is."

"They supported themselves. They didn't need government handout from men like you. Who would later return and take their assets for your own self?"

Kex laughs. Gesturing a point.

"For a titagod, you know your human politics."

From the door, Stephanie and Alex sneak by, seeing The Powerman and Kex inside the office.

"We have to keep moving, Stephanie."

"Not until we know what they're talking about."

"We could just go in there, you know."

Stephanie glares at Alex and smiles.

"That's a good idea. The best you've had all day."

Stephanie attempts to open the door, before she could do so, Beatrice approaches them.

"What are you two doing here?"

"We came to speak with Mr. Kendrick." Stephanie said. "We're from the Enigma News Office."

"Oh, I get it. Press. Well, he has an important visitor in there with him right now. You'll have to wait."

"No kidding." Alex said. "The Powerman is in there."

Beatrice stares at him. Stephanie turns her eyes toward him with annoyance. He shrugs his shoulders and holds his hands up.

"Sorry. Too much information?"

The Powerman and Kex continue their rugged conversation with one another. Powerman starts asking Kex questions that concern with Zeus and his recent tests. Kex laughs as he stares at Powerman, walking up to him.

"Yes. Me and the King of the gods have an agreement."

"An agreement to get rid of me."

"Yes. I need you gone. Don't you understand? With you gone, I can take back this city. A city that has lost its way. We live in a world that has already lost its way. Because of you, that damn ninja up north along with some revived soldier, that armored man, and some god from another realm. All of you are the problem. The real problem with the world. Playing gods as if you're all God. I have news for you, Taltus. You're not God. You damn heroes are not God. You're all false gods. Looking to be tossed away into the flames and I will be the one to do so."

The Powerman snatches Kex by his shirt, holding him up off his feet. Beatrice sees it and runs to the door, Alex moves over, standing in the way.

"Get out of my way, boy!"

"What can you do against him, huh?"

"Yeah. He's right. What can you do against The Powerman?" Beatrice scoffed.

The Powerman held up Kex, staring him in the eyes. Kex grinned in the face of The Powerman.

"Go ahead and do it." Kex demanded.

"Do what?"

"Kill me and prove to the world that I am right about you heroes. False gods! All of you. Prove it to me, prove it to them, and more importantly, prove it to yourself. You're worthless. You're all worthless."

A bright light flashes in the office. From the light emits Zeus, in his full form. Standing in the office with both The Powerman and Kex Kendrick. Stephanie, Alex, and Beatrice can see Zeus in the office, and they are terrified.

"Is that who I think it is?" Beatrice said.

"Yes. Its Zeus, the Greek god of thunder." Stephanie said.

"Holy shit!" Alex said.

Zeus stood still, facing The Powerman as he continues holding Kex up above him, preparing to strike him.

"Put him down, Taltus."

"Go away, Zeus. Before I finish you off next."

"You couldn't even if you tried. You want these tests to end? Fine. Face me and end my life to end these tests."

Powerman sat Kex on the floor. Kex ran over to the other side of his desk to avoid the two mighty forces. Zeus and The Powerman stare down.

"Are you ready to die, Taltus?"

"I won't fight you here. There're too many lives at stake. I want to end you where no humans will be occupied."

Zeus nodded. He blinked.

"You're love for humanity has made you soft. Very well, to a land where no humans are occupied."

Zeus and Powerman both disappear through a bright light. Beatrice bolts into the office with Stephanie and Alex behind her. She approaches Kex, who sat down in his chair.

"Sir, are you alright?"

"I've never felt better, Beatrice."

Beatrice turns around, seeing Stephanie and Alex behind her.

"You have some more visitors, sir."

Kex turns in the chair, looking at Stephanie and Alex. He proceeds Beatrice to let them stay, so he could talk with them. Beatrice obeys Kex's command and exits the office.

Out in a mountain region, The Powerman and Zeus beam out from the light. Powerman scouts the area, seeing nothing but mountains around him. He looks toward Zeus, who is already prepared.

"This will do." The Powerman said.

"Good. I hope you've said your goodbyes."

"I won't need to."

IV

A TITAGOD'S STRENGTH

The Powerman and Zeus do battle in the mountain region far away from Enigma City. The two fight each other as if it was their last day, fighting for their last breath. Both of them throwing blows at one other. Zeus starts throwing lightning bolts at Powerman, who blocks them with his hands and his lightning vision. Powerman tackles Zeus down to the ground. On the ground, Powerman raises up a boulder, smashing it onto Zeus' head. Zeus shakes off the impact. He grins, kicking Powerman across the mountain.

"You haven't learned anything, Taltus!"

Zeus grabs a handful of The Powerman's cape, throwing him against the mountains, flying completely through it, leaving a hole in the mountain as Zeus flies toward him.

"You don't understand, Taltus. I am the King of the gods. I am the ruler of Mount Olympus!"

Zeus stomps Powerman into the ground, smearing his white suit with dirt and blood and tearing his dark blue cape. Zeus continues stomping The Powerman more and more, waiting for him to attack. Powerman flies away from the incoming stomp and punches Zeus. He takes a hold of Zeus' hair and slams him against the mountains.

He slams Zeus continually until he sat still. Powerman hovers into the air, staring at Zeus.

"This ends now!"

The Powerman dives down toward Zeus like a missile preparing to strike. Powerman spears Zeus through the mountain, causing the mountain to collapse completely atop the two of them. The mountain remains as nothing but rock and rubble, Through the dirt-filled air, The Powerman rises up from the debris. He searches for Zeus through the rubble and doesn't find him. Not even a hint of him anywhere.

"He escaped."

The Powerman flies away from the destroyed mountain and out of the region.

After several days of passing, Kex and Beatrice enter a limo, the driver turns to Kex, asking him where he is heading. Kex looks at the driver.

"To the airport. I have some business up in Retropolis."

"What business do you have up in Retropolis, Kex?" Beatrice asked.

"I have a meeting with a woman who is dying to meet me. She says she has a grand plan that can solve all our problems."

"What is the woman's name?"

"I don't know yet. Though, I hear she is pale and somewhat ecstatic. Sometimes crazy they say. You don't know what she's going to do next."

"Are you prepared for confronting her?"

"Beatrice, this woman and I share a common goal that will eradicate our common enemies. This is what I've been waiting for to happen."

The limo drives away from the KexInc. building.

In the Enigma News Office, Stephanie reads up on some news from Newark, New Jersey that states the armored man, known as The Nano Man has saved the city from a group of religious fanatics as well as some Beast roaming the northern woods in Canada. She shakes her head.

"There's always a story somewhere." She said.

Within the walls of the Fortress of Cytron, Taltus sat, looking through a device which enabled him to see around the world. He scanned the world for the individuals whom Kex mentioned and set out to find them. Searching for any closest to Enigma City. Through the device, Taltus discovered himself staring at the city of Retropolis. What he could see in the device is a figure, standing atop a building, wielding a sword and cloaked in a hood. Reading up on the mythological vigilante who resided in the area. Known as The Swordman.

"I'm going to have to visit this myth myself."

Strangely, A large object had been floating through stellar space and appeared to be burning from all corners. The object itself a planet and it is sitting in a far galaxy. On the planet is a figure with a dark blue hood, overlooking a holographic image of a world. Giggling to himself.

"The Master will be pleased as to what we have discovered. There's a black hole hungry for this planet called Earth."

THE NANO MAN
WRATH OF THE THETAN

I

WE WATCH YOU, WE LEARN YOU

After battling and defeating the man called the Geier in the downtown area of Newark, New Jersey, Nathan Hawke, known as The Nano Man, traveled his way downtown for a press conference, involving his company and its future in the tech business. The conference building is crowded with business investors and numerous media crews. Representatives from other companies such as Clark Enterprises, KexInc., Glasco, Inc are also present at the event. The crowd stood, waiting for Nathan to arrive and present himself inside.

Down the street is Nathan inside a car driven by his chauffeur, Brian. Sitting next to Nathan is his assistant, Alice. She sat, reading a few papers that detailed the plan of Hawke's company for the next few years. She noticed there were deals made between Hawke Industries and Clark Enterprises.

"You didn't tell me about this." Alice said. "When was this deal made?"

"Sometimes I believe." Nathan said. "Trust me, it will do

wonders for the company. For both companies actually."

"You do understand that when this all comes full effect, things will have to change around the company, right?"

"Oh yeah. I am fully aware of the changes to come, Ms. Jacobs."

Nathan looked outside the window, seeing the conference building up ahead. He turned to Brian.

"How much further is the place? I can see it right there."

"You'll be there in just a few minutes, Mr. Hawke." Brian said. "Besides, I thought you didn't want to attend this conference event."

"Oh, I don't. I'm just going there to tease the people and make them love me. Simple solution with the public."

Alice gazed at Nathan, who's reaching into his jacket pocket, seeing him pulling out the device that communicates with his Nano Man tech. She taps him on his shoulder, getting his focus off the Nano Man business and back to the conference business.

"I trust that you won't be needing the armor at an event like this."

"Are you sure about that, Alice? Anything can happen in there. Someone could try to shoot me or even tackle me off of the stage. A fall off of a stage can and will injure you. The injury could and will most certainly be critical. I just like being prepared."

Alice kept her eyes on Nathan as he slowly put the device back into his pocket. He held his hand up toward her, smiling.

"See. It's not in my hand. It's in my pocket. Is that ok for you?"

"It will do just fine."

From several minutes, they arrive at the conference event. Brian exits the car first to open the door for Alice. She exits the car, waving at the attendees surrounding the place and waved at the media crew. Brian walks over to the other side of the car and opens the door for Nathan, who exits the car as if he was a rock star. Smiling with his sunglasses on. His arms up in the air. A smile on his face.

"Now, this is beautiful." Nathan said.

Blowing kisses to the women around him. Alice walked over to him, seeing him smiling and enjoying the moment.

"I can see they love me."

"They love you, alright. Love you enough to get as much from you as possible."

"Now that is harsh, Alice. Very harsh."

"That ego of yours is still growing?"

"That's not the only thing growing on me."

She shook her head in shame at Nathan, while he continues blowing kisses and shaking hands. Brian follows them into the building, where inside stood almost over one hundred and fifty people from across the world. Many come from other corporations and some are aspiring investors into the companies. Nathan glances around the interior of the building, spotting Glasco, Inc. and KexInc. logos on chairs and tables.

"I'm surprised they gave us some furniture."

"They did that because they have their people here too. They want to know what you're planning for the company. Competition at its finest."

"I welcome competition, Alice. You know John D. Rockefeller said competition was a sin. He had a point. But, I prefer competition in this field. Keeps me hungry for more of what can be created or built."

They enter the main section and find their seats. The event has begun with the presenter speaking about the companies that have attended the event. Nathan looks around, searching for the other CEOs. He gazes around the corners of the room. He turns to Alice, questioning.

"Where are the CEOs?"

"They're somewhere around here, Nathan. Just focus on yourself for right now. You're about to go up on the stage."

"Uh huh. Yeah."

The presenter finally calls up Nathan, who stood up in his chair and looks at everyone in the room that he could see. Smiling and waving as he walks down the aisle toward the stage as if it's a red carpet event. Walking up the steps of the stage, he shakes the presenter's hand and stands behind the podium with his company logo on the front. He savors the small moment. He looks out in front of him, seeing nothing but a sea of people, wearing suits and ties.

"I can only see suits, so I'm taking that as an ok, I can talk now."

The audience laughs. Nathan smiled at them and took a gaze to Alice.

"We are here for a plethora of things. Business investing, company agreements. Deals to be made. Friendships to begin anew, trust to grow. Hell, backs to be stabbed and who else knows what goes on behind the scenes in some of the companies, huh."

Nathan laughs while the audience remains quiet. Some giggles are heard responding to Nathan's choice of humor. Alice and Brian shake their heads.

"But, anyway. You are all here to hear me speak about my company, Hawke Industries and the future plans of making this company grow into a larger and stronger force in the field of business."

The audience applauds for a moment with Nathan smiling, seemly getting their attention on the matter.

"The plans I have in mind for the company will transcend it into the far future of beyond. A beyond land I would call it. Though, I already have similar business agreements planned and in full workings with the companies of Clark Enterprises and KexInc. Though I like its full name better, Kendrick

Corporations."

Nathan looks out for the CEOs of the two companies. Not spotting them in the audience. He smirked.

"It would seem to appear that Mr. Clark and Mr. Kendrick are not here today. They must be out on some important business matters. As more of us are on a daily basis I would presume."

Hawke discusses his plans of creating new tech that would change the foundation of the energy business entirely. He also speaks of the possibility for using nanotech robots on the battlegrounds for the military during warfare instead of humans. Stating that they've lost too many lives in the act of war. He also brought up the Nano Man. Saying,

"The Nano Man is a preview of the world to come. A world where humans will no longer be needed in the act of war. Instead, entities like the Nano Man will be the basis for human warfare."

Nathan thanks the audience and ends the conference event with it. While he and Alice were preparing to leave after speaking with several potential investors of the company who are enticed and excited about his business plans, partially the energy plan, three men in suits with gold ties and sunglasses approach him. Nathan looks at them. Business investors he believes. He extends his hand toward them.

"Pleasure to meet the three of you."

The men stood still as Nathan pulls back his hand. Not friendly he assumes.

"I take it you guys are foreigners, right. You don't shake hands in your country. I can understand."

"We are not exactly foreigners according to your vocabulary, Mr. Hawke." One of the men said.

"Then may I ask who you are?"

"We are the Elders. Elders of the Church of the Thetan.

We've come to have a word with you and you alone."

"Are you looking for some sort of handout. Some kind of idea of building a new church somewhere?"

"We don't want your money. We want you and your talent."

"I'm sure my talent can help you in the best of ways." Nathan smirks. "Contact my office and make an appointment. We can discuss deals there."

"We're not here for business matters. We know who you are. Truly."

"Of course, you do. I said my name and everything up on the stage. Hell, my name is plastered all over this building."

"We know of your activities. Your secret activities."

"My activities of dancing and humbling women? I'm sure it gets its way around."

"Not those earthly matters. We know you're the Nano Man."

Nathan stops laughing and remains quiet. Trying to calm himself from the inside.

"How do you know about that?" He questioned.

"We know everything there is to know about you. We have watched you and we have learned you, Mr. Hawke. Which is why we have a proposition for you this day."

"What proposition?"

"Come to our church and all your answers will be given unto you. That, I can assure you fully."

The men turn around and leave. Nathan stands by himself, trying to absorb in all he has heard from the men. Alice walks over to him, seeing concern in his face.

"Something wrong, Nathan?"

"No… There's nothing wrong. Tell me, what do you know of the Church of the Thetan?"

II

SPEAKING WITH THE ELDERS

Nathan sits inside his Nano-Bunker, researching all he can about the Elders and the Church of the Thetan. He continually searches from the time after he came back from the conference event till the moon was shining down on the Hawke Mansion in the clear night sky. Alice walked into the bunker, seeing him at the computer monitors.

"It's dark and you're still at it?"

"Yes I am. I can't find hardly anything about the church. They told me to come over there to find out what they know about me. They know I'm the Nano Man. They could know much more than I possibly don't even know."

"Just give it some time. Don't try to rush things ahead of yourself. You know that tends to go bad for you."

"Only when I don't have a follow-up plan."

"Do you? Have a follow-up to this whole thing?"

Nathan glances over to the Nano Man suit standing nearby. Nathan is mesmerized by the suit. Alice turns and sighs, placing her hand on her head.

"So what. You're just going to go in there, blazing energy beams at them. Expecting them to give you all they know about you?"

Nathan sat quietly. Taking in what Alice had said to him.

69

After a moment of silence, Nathan looks toward Alice. Looking into her eyes, seeing how she's worried about him.

"Yes."

Alice holds her head down and left the bunker. Nathan slowly turns back to the monitors, researching further and he later finds an address to the church in Newark. He smiled.

"Looks like I'll be seeing you tomorrow."

Nathan turned off the monitors and left the Nano-Bunker.

"First thing in the morning."

In the morning, Nathan prepares himself for going to the church. In the living room of his mansion stands Alice, waiting on Nathan to enter the room. Nathan walks down the stairs into the living room, seeing Alice waiting on him.

"Uh. Morning, Alice."

"Morning to you as well."

Nathan steps off the stairs, walking over to her. He hugs her and kisses her on the cheek.

"I know where you're going, Nathan."

"How did you find out? You were spying on me last night after you left? What did you place in the bunker? Some kind of secret microphone?"

"I overheard you saying 'first thing in the morning'. That told me you're about to go over there now."

Nathan sighs.

"I am. I need to know what they know about me."

Alice exhales slowly. Nathan stares at her. Trying to cheer her up a bit with a cheeky smile.

"I will be fine. Don't worry about it."

"Just make sure you're at the office for the business discussion."

Alice walks out of the room, towards the door.

"I will be there. I promise you."

Alice looks back to Nathan, showing a faint smile as she leaves the mansion.

Nathan drives himself through the city of Newark, searching for the address of the church. Finding himself driving almost out of the main city limits, he sees a building up ahead. The building appeared to be a large cathedral with white and gold lining and symbols mounted on it. Nathan drove closer and recognized the symbol on top of the building.

"This is the place."

Nathan parks his car, walking towards the building. Seeing no one standing outside or nearby. He approaches the large wooden doors, pushing them open. The doors open slowly with a creaking sound to follow. Inside, Nathan sees what appears to be an average church. The pews and podium in place with a large Scientology symbol on the wall behind the podium stage. The doors shut and Nathan turns back at them. He glances around, seeing one of the men from the conference standing in front of him. Nathan jolts when he sees the man.

"Did I frighten you, Mr. Hawke?"

"Somewhat. You could've just said hi, welcome to the church of such and such."

"The Church of the Thetan is the name of this place."

"Good to hear. I came to hear what you and your two buddies know of me. You said that if I was to come here, you would give me the answers that I seek."

"The answers are here. Waiting for you to accept them, Mr. Hawke."

The man walks down the aisle, looking back to Nathan. Nathan stands still. Calm.

"Follow me."

"I'm not sure about that, pal." Nathan said gesturing his hand.

"Follow me and get your answers or exit this place and remain in curious ignorance."

"I'm not ignorant." Nathan mentioned.

Nathan decides to follow the man down the aisle, towards the back of the church. The back was covered with symbols and designs focused on the church's faith and their designs. Nathan looks around, unaware and unknown of the church and their belief system.

The man leads Nathan into a small room where three seats were positioned. Two of them were already occupied by the other two men, leaving only one for the man to approach and which he sits. The men face Nathan, standing in the middle of the room, facing them.

"What is this? Some kind of council meeting?"

"You could say that."

"May I learn of my answers now, please."

The men gaze at one another, turning to Nathan. They nod.

"Finally."

"The answers you seek are here for you, Mr. Hawke." The left man said. "What you do with them is at your own cost and your own judgment."

"The answers will shape the foundations of your life, your company, and all who are around you." The man on the right said.

"Are you ready for them, Mr. Nathan Hawke?" The middleman said.

"I am. Let it all out already."

"We know who you truly are Nathan Hawke. We know of your birth, your home schooling, your intellect, your talents, your thoughts and ideas. You seek to change the future. To make it better than those before you have tried. You called your plans, a beyond land. Something that you dream of on a daily basis. You sit inside your Nano-Bunker, designing new suits of the Nano Man. In all shapes and fashions."

"You seek to have one that will enable space travel, one that will allow you to go to the depths of the seas, one that will give you enhanced strength of a beast. Your future is bright. You know this as well as we. But, with all is a weakness and a cost. There is something you lack inside yourself. Something far more powerful than tech and machinery."

"What do I lack that seems to hold me back on the future I intend to create?"

"Your spirit."

Nathan stared at him with confusion showing on his face. As if he doesn't understand what he said to him.

"My spirit?"

"You lack a spiritual power and focus within you. Without it, you won't be able to create the future you intend to present to the modern world."

"Ok. This is getting out of hand. I'm not interested in joining your church or becoming one of you elders, alright. Seems I got my answers and I will be leaving you all now."

"No, you will not."

The doors shut on Nathan. He looks back to the Elders. Not amused.

"Let me out!" Nathan yelled.

"Not until you hear our proposition. The one we told you about at your event."

"I thought the proposition was for me to come here and receive the answers I sought out."

"No. The proposition is much higher than that."

"Well, what is it and how is it higher than my answers?"

"We want you to be our leader. Our Operating Thetan."

"I don't understand. Why me?"

"Because we see the potential within you. But, in order to become our leader, you must first defeat our current leader, Zaro."

"Where is this Zaro now?"

"He is at our secret location. Awaiting your answer to the proposition we have given you. He is aware of the task you have before you."

"Where is this place of secrecy?"

"You will know when you accept the proposition. Take your time. For you only have until the noon of the following day to accept."

"Why the morrow?"

"Because we do not like to waste time on important matters. Think it over through the night, Mr. Hawke and make your decision. Show up to the location or don't. The choice is yours and yours alone."

The doors open behind Nathan. He turns, looking, seeing an opportunity to leave. The middle Elder extends his hand toward the doors.

"You may leave now."

"Thank you. I will consider the offer."

Nathan walks out of the room, leaving the church.

Hours later, Nathan sits inside the Nano-Bunker with Alice and Rick Carter, a close friend of his from the military. Nathan tells them about the Elders and the answers they told him. He also spoke to them of the proposition that was given to him. To become the Elders' new leader. Their Operating Thetan. Alice looks at Nathan, not liking what she is hearing, and Rick stands still, quiet. Sinking in all Nathan was telling them.

"So, they chose you to be their new leader?" Rick said.

"Their Operating Thetan you're saying?"

"That's right. I do know much of anything about their church or their beliefs. They knew me very, very well. They believe I can be their leader and bring about the future that I've always talked about. The Beyond Land. A land where energy would be free to all on the earth. Unlimited power."

"But, they want you to fight against their current leader." Alice said. "What makes you think this isn't some kind of set-up?"

"Because they were serious. Completely serious. If I choose to do this, they will send me the address of the location. I go there, confront their leader and defeat him. Making me their new leader. They would obey whatever I command them to do."

Alice sighs. Rick nods his head.

"Do what you feel is right, Nate." Rick said. "This is your decision to make. Not ours."

Nathan smiles.

"Thanks, Ricky."

"Don't call me that, man. Call me Rick. Just Rick will do."

Nathan looks at Alice. Waiting for her to response to him with an answer of her own.

"Just as long as you don't kill yourself doing this kind of stuff."

Nathan laughs.

"I wouldn't go there in a suit or jeans and a t-shirt."

"What would you go there wearing?" Rick said. "They have some kind of dress code you're supposed to follow?"

"I don't know. I was referring to wearing the Nano armor."

"At least you won't immediately die if things go wrong." Alice said.

"That is the idea."

In the secret site, Zaro sits at a table with some other elders around him. Wearing a light brown attire with his shaven head. A grim look. They hear a knock at the door, aware and prepared. Zaro stands up from the table. Commanding one of the Elders to open the door. The Elder opens the door and standing at the door was Niles Valcrow. He looked at the Elders and gazed toward Zaro.

May I enter according to your will?"

"Yes. Please enter in, Mr. Valcrow." Zaro said. "I have been expecting you for a while now."

Niles enters the building as the Elder closes the door. Zaro extends his hand toward the table, where he and Niles sat.

"I hear you spoke to the Geier inside the prison?"

"I did. He is already aware of the real plans around here."

"I can see that from his actions in the city."

"So, when is he coming?"

"Who?"

"Your boss?"

"He will come when he decides to come."

"I can't be running around these places like a chicken with his head cut off. People will begin to notice things."

"Then make them go unnoticed. We are here to serve our true leader and our god. Not men in suits and ties. Wearing smelling liquids on their clothing to appease the opposite sex."

"You making a mockery at my cologne?"

"Yes. Yes, I am. Anyhow, if Hawke decides to show up here to battle me, you can be assured that my boss will be here by then. That way, you can speak with him about your little plans."

Niles grins. Staring a hole through Zaro. He stands up from the table.

"Thank you for the short talk, Operator."

Niles turns away, leaving through the door. Zaro sits at the table, thinking to himself with his eyes closed. Rubbing his hands together slowly.

Past midnight, Nathan was alone in the bunker, meditating on his decision. Passing the hours, meditating, Nathan stands up, walking over to the monitor. On the monitor was a message for him. He opens the file, detailing it came from an anonymous source. The message was the address to the location of Zaro. Nathan nods with a smirk and he stands up from his seat, walking over to approach the Nano Man armor. He opens the sealed door of the closet.

The armor came sliding out of its holding place. Nathan smiles. With the help of his machinery, Nathan put on the armor. The armor shines the bunker with its midnight teal and silver coloring, surging with power from its nuclear reactor. The helmet set itself down over Nathan's face. Closing from the sides and lastly from the top.

"Here I come." Nathan said.

The armor charges up as the bunker's aerial doorway opens, allowing him to fly out. He did so, flying toward the location site. The Nano Man was coming to confront Zaro.

III

HERE GOES, THE THETAN

Zaro stands inside the secret location building, waiting for Nathan's arrival. From the doors enter some of the Elders, running towards him with a message to deliver. Zaro turns to them with intensity in his face.

"What do you have for me?"

"Nathan Hawke has received the message. He's on his way here as we speak to you."

Zaro smiles.

"Prepare the site. Let's give him more to see. Also, make sure the area is open for the boss. For he is also on his way here."

"Yes, our Operator."

The Elders leave Zaro in the room by himself. Zaro exhales, preparing himself for the fight. Zaro walks over to a closet. Opening the closet, Zara sees a set of armor. Similar to the armor of the ancient Romans. Zaro takes the armor, putting it on, covering his body and head. For he knew Nathan would come with his Nano Man armor on and prepared for the fight.

Meanwhile, Nano Man flies through the air at high speed. Inside his helmet, Nathan followed a trail that will lead him to the location.

"Only a few miles ahead."

Nano Man flies to the location. Zaro was fully prepared, inside a room he calls the 'determination room', which was the room where he and Nathan would have their battle to determine which of them will be the leaders of the Elders.

"When will he be here?" Zaro said.

"We've caught him in the sir, Operator." An Elder said. "It won't be much longer now."

"Let it not be."

After several minutes of waiting and Zaro's patience slowly about to run out. He paces through the room in waiting for Nathan's arrival. From the outside, they hear something crash into the ground from the air. Zaro walks. He stands in the middle of the room, smiling. He knows what caused the crashing sound.

"He has arrived."

The Elders open the two doors at the front, revealing The Nano Man, standing. He stares at the Elders, looking ahead of them, seeing Zaro in the room. Nano Man enters the room as the Elders exit, closing the doors behind them.

"I am here." The Nano Man said. "I take it you must be this Zaro guy."

"That would be me." Zaro said. "I see that you have accepted the proposition that was offered to you. Smart decision you have made this night."

"The idea seemed to peak my interest. So, if you don't mind my beating your ass in front of your elders, let's get this fight started."

"I've been waiting for this moment."

Zaro lunges at Nano Man like an animal, slamming him against the wall and immediately punching him in the head, trying his hardest to crack open the helmet. Nano Man blocks the next incoming punch and headbutts Zaro. Zara stumbles and Nano Man grabs him by the shoulders, throwing him across the room

Zaro slams into the wall, cracking the window. He lays on the ground for a moment before getting to his feet. Nano Man hovers toward him and spears Zaro through the sets of tables in the room. Nano Man holts Zaro up and slams him through the remaining table. Zaro lays on the ground as Nano Man begins pummeling him to the ground. Inside the helmet, the suit picks up an unknown energy that is surrounding Zaro.

"What kind of energy is this? I've never seen anything like it before."

"Because as the Elders told you." Zaro said quietly. "You lack a spirit."

Zaro knees and kicks Nano Man off of him, stomping his head into the floor. He continues stomping on the helmet, hearing the sound of boot meeting metal. Zaro grins at what he's doing. He places his boot over Nano Man's helmet. Holding it in place.

"How could you lead them without a spirit?" Zaro questioned. How could you become an Operating Thetan without a spirit?"

"Innovation." Nano Man said, as the helmet eyes glow brighter. "That is the key to leadership."

Grabbing Zaro's boot, Nano Man kicks him in the gut before hovering himself off the ground. Hovering in the air, he tackles Zaro against the wall. He tackles him again against the wall and spears him until he fell down to one knee. Nano Man stood in front of Zaro with his hands out, preparing to blast him with an energy beam. Zaro stares at him.

"You have your opportunity, Nathan Hawke. Do what must be done. Defeat me and win the Elders to do your bidding. Become their new Operating Thetan."

Nano Man was silent, not even a flinch in his body. He slowly closes his hands. Zaro exhales and scoffs at Nano Man.

"Ok." Nano Man said.

He opens his hands, blasting two energy beams at Zaro,

destroying his armor and knocking him out from the strength of the blasts. He gazes outside the windows, seeing the sun beginning to rise. With Zaro's defeat, the Elders enter the room, surrounding Nano Man. He watches their every move and the Elders stop in place, bowing down before him. Catching him off guard, he attempts to leave the building, but the front doors open on their own. As if a gust of wind blew them open. Someone was standing at the door, covered in the shadows.

"You have done well, Nathan Hawke." The voice in the shadows said. "You have defeated Zaro. My finest lieutenant. Making yourself in his place. Wonders will come from this."

"Who are you?" Nano Man said.

The figure walks out of the shadows. Standing tall and wearing ancient garbs and a white cloak. He faces Nano Man with no fear. The Elders even tremble at his presence, bowing before him in total fear. The Nano Man was the only one standing in the room besides the figure.

"You are the Elders' new Operating Thetan. Allow me to introduce you to myself. I am The Thetan."

"The Thetan? The actual one?"

"I am the one and only. I am above all the other thetans that have come across over the centuries. I am the one true Thetan. My spirit is more powerful than you can ever imagine and the power that comes with it can be shown with a great feat."

"Why have you come here? To see your lieutenant defeat me and take me out?"

"No. I have come to see which of you would be the victor of the bout. I see now that it is you who have won. I am here to give you the opportunity of a lifetime. You have two options standing before you, Nathan Hawke."

"What are these two options of yours?"

"You can accept your new place as Operating Thetan, which will make you my new lieutenant."

"What's the second option?"

"The second option is you decline the offer of being my lieutenant and I will see to it that Newark is destroyed along with you. If you decline, I will personally kill you and make sure your city is in flames and all who live within it are buried beneath the rubble."

"Is that right?"

"Choose your decision wisely, Nathan Hawke. Think of others before thinking of yourself on this one. For you do not have much of a choice."

Nano Man thought to himself. He thought carefully of the two choices placed in front of him. In one, he could become a leader of an unknown amount of men, all who would do what he commands of them and become the lieutenant of The Thetan, a spiritual man of great power and might. The other decision, he could decline The Thetan's offer and face the possibility of meeting his death as well as the deaths of all who live in Newark. He thought and thought.

"I have come to a decision, Thetan."

"What is your decision, Nathan Hawke. Speak of it now before I choose your decision myself."

"As much as I like to have an army of my own. I always said that I prefer robots in the act of war, not humans. The Elders are human beings. If they were to fail, it would be because of my decisions and choices. I don't need any more humans dying because of me. I pick the second option. I decline your offer."

The Thetan laughed at Nano Man. Clapping his hands.

"The second option you have chosen, Nathan Hawke. I hope you're prepared for what's about to come to you."

"I am. Do what you can. But know this, I will stop you at any cost."

"You stop me! I am The Thetan. I am beyond your feeble comprehension!"

The Thetan disappeared in thin air. Nano Man made his stance, circling around him, looking for The Thetan to appear in his eyesight. The helmet cannot pick up The Thetan's trace.

"Where is he?"

The Thetan reappears through the thin air, knocking Nano Man through the wall with a right haymaker. The haymaker was powerful, it made a dent in the Nano Man armor. The Thetan walks outside through the large hole in the wall, raises up his arms. He gazes above him into the sky. His eyes shut. Nano Man watches him.

"I call on you, Xenu, my god. Give me the strength and the power to kill Nathan Hawke and destroy his city of Newark, New Jersey! Aid me in this battle, my god. Aid me."

Nano Man stands up on his feet, facing The Thetan. Mentally preparing himself for the fight that may cost him his life and the lives of many others.

IV

NANOTECH VS. EXTRATERRESTRIAL

The Nano Man and The Thetan fight one other across the site. The Thetan is seemly overpowering Nano Man due to his prayer to his god, Xenu. The Thetan stomps Nano Man in his chest, into the ground, pushing the reactor closer to Nathan's heart.

"Your tech cannot match the power of the spiritual feats."

"Maybe not. But I can match its strength till my dying breath."

The Nano Man shoves The Thetan's boot from his chest, flying towards him, tacking him in the abdomen and flying up in the air. Nano Man held him tightly as The Thetan started beating him in the back. The Thetan extended his fingers, placing them on Nano Man's back.

"This will send you back to the ground."

The Thetan yells as lightning bolts were coming from his fingers, covering the Nano Man armor and injecting itself into the armor's power core. Nano Man noticed the helmet going out and himself slowly beginning to fall from the air.

"This cannot be happening!"

"It is happening, Nathan Hawke. You have no other options now."

Nano Man starts to fall toward the ground. He attempts

firing energy beams at The Thetan, the beams wouldn't cooperate with Nathan's demands due to the power outage. The Thetan laughs as the both of them were falling.

"It seems that you will meet your death from a sky fall. While I, on the other hand will levitate myself from the ground's rough impact."

The Thetan levitates himself, hovering into the air, watching Nano Man fall and collapse onto the ground below. The Thetan grins. He makes his way down to the ground where Nano Man lays, nearly unconscious from the impact of the fall. The armor is cracked and beaten down.

"What can you do, Nathan Hawke." The Thetan said. "What can you do?"

Inside the Hawke Industries building, Alice walked through the offices, not finding Hawke. Rick walked by and she stopped him.

"Sorry, but have you heard from Nathan in the last few hours?"

"No. I thought you were with him. Where is he?"

"I don't know."

"Let's go look for him"

Preparing themselves to go and search for Nathan, walking down the hall, Niles approaches them from the elevator, smiling.

"I'm sorry, Ms. Jacobs and Mr. Carter. But, I was wondering have the both of you heard from Nathan?"

"No sir." Alice said.

"We haven't heard a word from him since last night."

Niles nods.

"Very well. See to it that you find him. We need him here and now."

Niles leaves them. Alice and Rick enter the elevator and

the door closes. Niles looks back, seeing the elevator door closing. He walks into his office, snatching his phone from the desk. Dialing a number, he waits impatiently for a response. The response on the other end of the phone picks up.

"Send your group of guys to follow Ms. Alice Jacobs and Mr. Rick Carter." Niles demanded. "Yes. Make sure they're taken care of. We cannot have them ruining our plans. Thank you."

Niles hangs up the phone. He sits down at his desk, staring at his computer monitor.

"Now, where is that data plan?"

Downstairs, Alice and Rick exit the building and enter the car with Brian sitting in the driver's seat. He looks back, seeing them entering the car. Confused.

"What's going on, Ms. Jacobs?" Brian asked.

"We need to go to Nathan's home. It's urgent."

"Ok."

Brian starts the car and drives off the company property, entering the street. Behind him are two sets of black SUVs, which followed him down the street from the office. Rick looks behind them, seeing the SUVs.

"Is it me or are we being followed?"

Alice turns, looking back at the SUVs. She catches the passenger reaching out of the window with a machine gun pointing toward them. She screams, ducking her head.

"Get down!" She yelled.

The passenger starts firing shots at them with Brian driving through the Newark traffic, running red lights and almost getting into wrecks to avoid a gunshot from the passenger in the SUV.

"What the hell is going on?!" Brian asked hastily. "I didn't expect to be getting shot at today. What has Nathan done this time?!"

"I don't know." Alice said. "I really have no idea."

The passenger continues shooting, Brian watches them from the car door mirror. He thinks to himself.

"I have an idea. Hold on."

Brian pushes down on the gas pedal, zooming pass other cars. He's coming up to a set of eighteen-wheeler trucks coming in his direction. Alice looks on, seeing the trucks up ahead.

"What are you about to do, Brian?"

"Trust me on this, Ms. Jacobs. We will survive this."

"I hope we do." Rick said.

Brian drives closer to the trucks with the SUVs inching closer on them. The SUV reaches the side of the car, ramming them, jolting Alice and Rick in the back. Brian keeps his eyes forward. Onward to the trucks.

"Hold on!"

Brian drives quickly past the trucks, entering his line of sight. He turns away from one of the trucks as it rams itself into the front of the SUV, killing both the driver and passenger. The second SUV was driving just as fast, running itself into the back of the first SUV. The cars around them were trapped by the sight of the wreckage collision. Brian makes a u-turn to get a closer look at the drivers. He passes by the sight and gazes toward the windows. Rick looks. He recognizes one of the drivers.

"I know that man."

"You do? From where?"

"From the office. He's one of Niles' men. Follows him everywhere he goes. Sort of like a secret protection group."

"You're saying Niles sent them to kill us?" Brian asked.

"Not you." Rick said. "Me and Alice. Because we went looking for Nate."

"Niles knows something we don't." Alice said. "We have to find out why. Still take us to Nathan's home. Just to check."

"Yes ma'am."

Brian leaves the sight as the police started to arrive near the wreckage sight.

Almost into the middle of nowhere, not far from the site, The Thetan is crushing Nano Man underneath his boot. Nano Man can barely fight back as his armor is slowly decreasing in power. The Thetan turns Nano Man over, grabbing his helmet, attempting to electrocute him through the helmet into his brain.

"Looks like your end has come, Nathan Hawke. Any final words?"

"Yeah." Nano Man said. "Thanks for stomping on the chest."

Nano Man raises up from the ground, punching The Thetan to the dirt. He glares up toward Nano Man, thinking and staring at him.

"How did you receive more power?"

"The armor found a way to absorb your energy. Something about that spiritual matter you were talking about has increased my armor even more than I thought it could reach. Thank you."

The Thetan went to lunge toward Nano Man, he hovers over The Thetan, snatching him by his cloak and tossing him into a nearby tree. He flew toward him and kicked him through the tree, leaving only the trunk remaining. The Thetan laid on the ground, covered in branches and leaves. Regaining his strength as Nano Man stood before him.

"I suggest you get to your feet, Thetan. Face me like you mean it."

"You dare mock me!"

The Thetan flies toward Nano Man. Nano Man does the same. He uppercuts The Thetan in the face and knees him in the gut, before elbowing him in his back, knocking him down.

"I will not be defeated." The Thetan said. "There's still a

chance for me to defeat you. Xenu, I command you aid me at once!"

The sky lights up. Nano Man looked toward the sky through the set of trees, so did The Thetan. From the sky comes down, Xenu, in full detail. The large alien figure wearing his cape that resembles the cape of Dracula. Nano Man took a step back. An alien deity in his presence. Something he has yet to come to believe.

"What in the hell is this? An alien wearing Dracula's cape? Now that is a story worth telling folks."

Xenu rams Nano Man through the forest, knocking him out of it. Xenu walks in the air above Nano Man, as did The Thetan.

"I need your power." The Thetan said. "I need it to defeat him."

"I gave you power and it wasn't enough?" Xenu said. "What have you become, my Thetan? What has happened to you to make you this… powerless?"

"I have done much over the centuries, master. I need more power to complete the tasks you have set out before me."

"I will deal with this human. After this, I will consider granting you more power needed to complete your quests on this earth and in this life."

Nano Man watches the two talk to one another. He stands, waving at them.

"Hey! I don't know if you're aware of this but, I'm still alive and kicking. Ready for another round, guys?"

Xenu stares at Nano Man with anger in his eyes.

"He seems to mock me! I will end this feeble light period!"

Xenu flies down toward Nano Man, looking for a final blow. Nano Man stands still, curving his arms as his chest starts to glow. Xenu inches closer to Nano Man as his chest enlarges itself.

"Ultrabeam!" Nano Man said.

The ultrabeam blasts from his chest, covering Xenu, knocking him down. The Thetan is lost for words. Astounded by seeing Xenu on the ground, with scorch marks on his body and his cape burned. The Thetan's eyes become intense toward Nano Man.

"I will end your life!" The Thetan said.

"Come on and try, ancient one." Nano Man said. "We don't have all day."

The Thetan flies into the sight of Nano Man. Coming closer, Nano Man extends his hands and stares at The Thetan, who was confused to Nano Man's choice of movement.

"The fight is over. I have won."

Nano Man shoots a series of energy beams at the Thetan. Increasing by the mixture of The Thetan's own spiritual energy. The level of strength from the beams are powerful enough to defeat The Thetan. The beams cease, Nano Man looks ahead, seeing The Thetan on the ground next to Xenu.

"The fight is done."

Xenu slowly raises up, staring at The Nano Man, who was preparing to blast them with another attack of energy beams. Xenu reaches over and holds back The Thetan.

"This is not over." Xenu said as he disappears along with The Thetan.

Nano Man gazes around, not seeing The Thetan or Xenu. He shrugs his shoulders.

"Time to go home now."

He flies into the air, returning to his mansion.

Brian arrived to Nathan's mansion. Stopping the beaten-down vehicle. Alice and Rick ran to the door. Entering the mansion, they begin searching for Nathan. Yelling out his name and going into nearly every room. Nathan's assistant, Derek Willis walks through the door. Alice sees him and approaches him.

"Hi, Derek."

"Morning to you, Ms. Jacobs."

"Sorry to have burst in. Have you seen, Nathan?"

"Not since last night of course. Said he was off on some business venture as always. You could check his bedroom."

They run to his bedroom. They reach the bedroom, not finding Nathan. Rick walks in and can hear the sound of running water coming from inside the bathroom.

"You hear that?" Rick said.

"I do." Alice replied.

Alice opens the bathroom door and see Nathan taking a shower. He turned, seeing Alice in the bathroom and Rick standing out by the door. Nathan stared.

"What the hell are you guys doing in here?"

"We came to see how you were." Alice said. "That's all."

Nathan stands quietly. Continuing his staring.

"Ok. Again, why are you still here?"

"I'm out." Rick said. "See you downstairs in the kitchen. I need a damn drink."

Alice turns to Nathan. Nathan continues his staring once more. He gestures to the shower.

"You want to join me or something. Because your eyes are saying something to me that's very unusual of you."

"No, I don't want to join you! Where were you?"

"You're asking me that right now? While I'm in the shower?"

"Yes, I am asking you about it!"

"I had to handle the Elder business."

"And have you handled it?"

"I did." Nathan smiled. "I'll explain more to you once I am out of the shower."

"Be sure you do."

"Close the door, please."

Alice slams the bathroom door, making Nathan laugh.

Finishing his shower, Nathan walks downstairs to the living room, seeing Alice sitting, waiting for him. Rick sits in the kitchen drinking on of Nathan's beers. Nathan gazes at him and the beer bottle.

"That's not what I think it is?" Nathan asked. "Is it?"

Rick held up the beer bottle.

"Drinking in the day are you?" Nathan said.

"After what I've been through so far and what I just seen, yeah, I need a drink right now."

Nathan walks toward Alice, sitting next to her on the couch.

"Explain yourself." Alice said.

"You sure about that?"

"I am very sure. Give me as much as you can possibly remember."

Nathan takes in a small breath before speaking. Rick stays at the kitchen table, ready to hear what Nathan has to say.

"Um. Well, I defeated the Elder's leader and afterwards meet the Thetan himself. The Thetan. Not some Operating one or any of the other kind. He gave me two choices, I could become the Operating Thetan, his lieutenant or I could decline and risk death for myself and the city. I chose the second and we fought to the death basically."

"This is not funny." Alice said.

"I haven't finished yet" Nathan mentioned. "Then, he summoned his alien god whose name is Xenu and we fought through the sky and forest. The two of them talked with each other and I defeated them both. Xenu took The Thetan with him to some place. I don't even know. Does that explain everything you wanted to know?"

Alice chose to remain silent, only an expression shown

toward Hawke. Nathan glances over to Rick who walks to the refrigerator, grabbing another beer bottle. Nathan shakes his head. Pointing to the bottles.

"You know you're going to buy me two more of those, right?"

"I'm sure of that." Rick said. Grabbing the second bottle.

"I'm taking the day off." Alice said. Standing up from the couch.

"So am I." Rick said. "I'll be drunk in a few hours anyhow. Forget all the shit that's happened in the last few hours."

"Ok. Um, Derek, make sure Rick gets all the beer he needs for the day."

"Yes sir."

"And make sure he pays us back for how many he drinks too."

"Will do, sir."

Nathan laughs to himself.

The following day, Nathan enters the company building, receiving a message. Someone was there to see him. Thrilled of having a visitor, he enters his office and inside the office was sitting, Kenari Clark, surprising Nathan.

"It's wonders to see you here." Nathan said. "Why are you here exactly? Especially at this time of the day?

"I wouldn't be here if it wasn't some urgent." Kenari said. "You know how I operate on certain matters."

"So, what is this urgent message you have to tell me? Is it something about our business partnership?"

"No. It has nothing to do with our companies."

Kenari hands Nathan a file, the file is titled *'The Resistance Protocol'*. Nathan intrigued by the title, opens the file and sees what is laid out inside. He nods his head with a confusing grin.

"You have got to be joking me."

"I'm not. Evan Nader told me to give it to you. Said you would have some sort of idea on what to do in this situation."

"So, Nader needs me to go talk with him? Him?"

"Yeah. I already have a list of possible recruits."

"Let's switch tasks."

"I wouldn't believe you'll like who's on my list to start with."

Nathan stares. Kenari grins at him humorously.

"Fair enough."

Kenari leaves out of the office. Looking back at Nathan, who's scanning through the file.

"See you around, Nate."

"Same here, Kenari."

Nathan lays the file on his desk, staring at it. He nods while looking through, reading the documents inside. He stares at the photos that were also placed in the file. Seeing things that were beyond his normal days.

"Next stop, T.I.T.A.N. Headquarters. Hope the Commander listens to me. I hear he likes to bark out orders."

COMMANDER NORLAND: SECTOR OF DARKNESS

I

MAKING AN ENTRY

Somewhere within the Korean Peninsula, sat a military base operated by a man named Kong Suk or as the natives know him as The Crimson Suk. Due to him casually wearing a red shroud over his face with a dark blue militaristic uniform and a red star on the left of his chest. Suk walked outside of the base and looked up. He continued to look up until he seen something moving in the air.

"Prepare the army." Suk said to one of his lieutenants.

"Why, sir? If I may ask."

"Because we have company coming and I want them to see what we have in store for them."

Suk looked in the air and seen what appeared to be an object flying. The object was indicating that it was coming closer toward the base with Suk standing in the front, watching the object becoming larger as it inched closer.

"I've been waiting for this moment."

The army ran out of the base in mass. They made a near perfect line, surrounding the base and covering Suk. He stood in front of them and paced in between the ones that were closer to him. He stopped in his steps and pointed up toward the object with the soldiers following his instructions to gaze up toward it.

"You see that in the air. That is T.I.T.A.N.'s little response team. They sent them here to take all of us out of the picture for power control. We will not surrender to their demands, verbally or physically. We will stand tall and we will overcome these rats."

The object is the Hoverjet with a T.I.T.A.N. Agent piloting the plane. The Hoverjet is an exclusive jet to T.I.T.A.N. that were designed by Nathan Hawke with his company's funding services. The jet is equipped with VTOL capabilities and turbojet engines.

Inside the plane is the response team of Woody Fields known as the Canadian Hawk, Steve Nixon, one of the United States' most amazing soldier, Andrea Pierson known as Whiplash, and their leader, Adam Watson known highly as Commander Norland. Norland approached the pilot.

"How soon will we land at the base?"

"Approximately eighty seconds."

Hawk grabbed his red and white shield from the jet wall and looked at Nixon preparing his firearms and Whiplash setting up her forearm whips, ready for the battle below.

"You two seem ready for this." Hawk said.

"Because we are, Fields." Nixon said. "I hope that we can do this job with no problems interfering."

"We'll get the job done." Whiplash said. "That's why we were chosen for this."

Hawk placed his shield on his left arm, making sure it fit. He looked around at the team inside the jet.

"Hey, did anyone tell you guys what T.I.T.A.N. was doing heading up into the northern parts of Canada?"

"No." Whiplash said. "No one told us about anything other than this mission we're on."

"That should be our only focus, Woody."

"I'm just curious. They were deeply silent on the matter. Not sure if it's some secret project they're working on."

"Everything's secret with T.I.T.A.N., Woody. You should at least know that."

Norland looked outside the window, seeing the base below. He walked toward the other team members, prepared for battle as they are."

"Are you ready?"

"YES SIR!"

"Good. Let's do this job and we can go on home, alright."

"Sure thing, boss." Hawk said. "We won't let you down."

Norland looked at Hawk. Smiling.

"When have any of you let me down."

"Never." said Nixon. "That's why we're here."

Norland nodded.

"Let's do this."

The Hoverjet is right above the base and above the soldiers. They try to contain themselves form the wind coming from the jet, making every attempt to stand still in their current space. Suk looked up at the base and raised up his fist toward it.

"Get out of your jet, fools and face all of us like the soldiers you deem yourselves to be!"

Inside the jet, Hawk looked through the window, seeing Suk with his fist in the air toward them and he could tell that he was yelling at them to come out of the jet and face them on the ground in battle. Hawk looked at Norland and pointed to Suk.

"May I ask why he's wearing a towel over his face?"

"It's not a towel, Woody."

"Then what is it? Because it looks like a towel. A simple, basic, red towel."

"It's a red hood." Norland said. "Matches the color of blood."

"Come again, boss?"

Nixon walked over to Hawk, concerned about his safety on the field and shaking his head in disturbance toward him.

"How about you ask him once we've captured the bastard."

"Yeah. I like that idea even better. Thanks Nixon."

The jet landed in the fields facing the base. Suk stood still with his arms crossed into his chest and the army prepared with their weapons facing the jet. The jet stood still and quiet.

The doors of the jet opened slowly like a ramp coming down on a stage. Suk stared deeply and was nearly without patience.

"Come on. Show yourselves to us."

The ramp came down and sat on the ground. From the darkness of the ramp came Norland and the team. They ran out with a fast pace straight for Suk and the soldiers. Suk caught them coming and he pointed toward them. The soldiers looked and yelled a cry for battle.

"Kill them!" Suk yelled.

The soldiers ran toward Norland and the team with Suk watching on, laughing to himself as the battle is about to begin. In front of them, Norland sees the army running toward them.

"The army is headed for us!"

"We're going to fight our way through them?" Hawk said.

"That's exactly what we're going to do."

Norland directed the team trop their field positions and ran toward the soldiers with force. Norland braced himself to the collision along with the others. The soldiers continued yelling toward them with their guns and blades up in the air. Norland inched closer toward the soldiers and took a small look around the area.

"You ready?!"

"WE ARE!" said the team.

"NOW!"

The team branched out and fought against the soldiers in different directions. Nixon took the left side of the soldiers with Hawk on his side, swiping through the soldiers with his shield as Nixon fired shots toward the heads of the soldiers. Whiplash took the right side on her own. She kicked and punched a few of the soldiers before having a small open space of her own. The soldiers near her area stopped and stared at her as they raised their guns toward her. She smiled.

"Allow me to show you my specialty in weaponry."

Whiplash held down her arms and from the forearms slid down a long whip made of titanium fabrics and was jolted with electricity that surged a reddish pink. The soldiers were confused at her choice of weapon. She yelled and started to whip and slash the soldiers through and through. Cutting some of their arms and hands off with their guns dropping to the dirt. The soldiers screamed at the pain they were feeling form the electric whips of Whiplash.

Norland rammed through the middle of the soldiers, seeking to get closer to Suk. He kicked back a few soldiers and punched many. He grabbed one soldier and raised him up above his head and threw him to the other soldiers running toward him, knocking them back as they fell to the ground. Norland reached to his side and pulled up his handgun, now shooting at the few soldiers in between him and Suk. While shooting the soldiers, Suk stood still as he moved his arms down to his side with his fists prepared for the coming fight. Norland fired the last shot at the remaining soldier. He fell down in front of Norland as he looked and faced Suk.

"It's all over, Kong Suk."

"This battle between us hasn't even sought to begin, Canadian!"

Suk quickly commanded his other soldiers to come out from the base and they ran toward Norland. Norland stood still and ready for soldiers' coming attack. The soldiers came closer and Norland decided to run toward them and immediately bashed through the entire pack of the soldiers. All the soldiers were knocked unconscious by the force of Norland's ram. Suk was appalled at the feat of Norland's strength and agility.

"Is that the best you can bring in battle, Suk?"

Suk reached to his back and pulled out a sword. He pointed it out toward Norland were fierce anger in his body language and his voice even presented the anger even more so than his stance.

"Enough of this! I'll handle these fools myself!"

Suk ran with anger toward Norland, who is already prepared for the attack. Suk swiped the sword at Norland, who took a step back. Suk continued to swipe the sword with Norland dodging and blocking the attacks with his armored forearms and boots. Suk began to swipe unknowingly in anger, letting it control him and get a hold over his fighting.

"I will not be defeated! I will not lose again a worm like you!"

Suk went for a stab and Norland grabbed the sword in between his arms and elbowed Suk in the face. Norland held the sword and slammed it against his leg, breaking the sword in half. He threw it down and walked toward Suk.

"Seems like you'll have to face me in hand-to-hand combat now."

"Ugh. Suit yourself."

Suk went for a left punch, Norland ducked the punch from Suk and pulled his arm back and delivered an uppercut to Suk, knocking him back as he stumbled to stand still and regain his balance. The force of the uppercut knocked the shroud and makeshift crown off of Suk's head. Suk felt to the ground on his knees, using his hands to cover up his face from Norland to see it.

"Afraid to show your face, Suk?"

Suk removed his hands from his face, revealing his disfigured and mutilated face. He yelled and lunged to attack Norland one more time. But, Norland moved out of the way, he grabbed Suk by his shoulders and slammed him down with a huge right haymaker. Suk slowly tried to stand up as Norland moves back and his eyes began to spark a light blue. Norland tried to regain his control with Suk still on the ground looking at him.

"The hell is wrong with this man?"

Norland looked up toward the sky. Snow started to fall upon the site.

"Let it fall." Norland said.

A blue lightning bolt, made of ice, came down from the sky and crashed down upon the base. Blowing the building up. Suk covered himself up to avoid further damage. The bolt and mist disappear slowly as Suk laid on the ground, not moving, but somehow, still breathing. The remaining soldiers stared at Norland and ran away from the site. Norland looked around at what happened, confused at his actions. The ream walked toward him and looked at him as if they were unaware of his unknown feats.

"What was that, boss?" Hawk said.

"I... I do not know, Woody. I have no idea where that came from."

"It looked like you summoned it, Commander." Nixon said. "I'm not sure how though."

"At least you cleared the field and we won this bout." Whiplash said. "That's what should matter."

"You're right about that, Andrea."

Norland looked and walked toward Suk and looked down at him, seeing him defeated and unable to fight back. Suk gazed up toward Norland with a fear in his eyes.

"I don't know what you are, but I surrender for now."

"As you should."

Norland grabbed Suk and picked him up to his feet. He walked him back to the hoverjet along with the team following them. Suk looked around at the decimated base and the dead soldiers that laid on the ground. Suk glared at Norland.

"This isn't over, Commander Norland. Things will happen once again with me at the center of it."

"I'm sure you'll dream about something in your prison cell."

They entered the jet and it hovered above the ground, flying away from the base site. Returning to T.I.T.A.N. Headquarters.

At the T.I.T.A.N. Headquarters, the agents congratulate Norland and the team on their victory in capturing Suk and defeating his army. They walked Suk to his cell, placing him inside and closing the door. Suk looked around and seen Norland standing at the door.

"You'll be in here for quite some time until they drop you off at Alcatraz or Ledger Haven."

"These walls won't hold me for very long, Commander. I will still have my victory."

"I'm sure you will succeed."

Norland walked away from the cell and looked around at the people walking through and through the base. Confused, Norland walked to the head office. Inside the office was no one. He left the office and went downstairs to Professor John Flm's laboratory. Norland entered the lab and Flm greeted him upon entry.

"Nice to see you today, Mr. Watson."

"I'm sorry to bother you at this time, Professor. Have you seen Colonel Nader anywhere?"

"I have not seen the Colonel since earlier today in the morning."

"Where did he go?"

"He led a small team of agents up north to the frozen areas of Canada."

"Why would he lead a team of agents up there. Didn't the US Military already make the attempt at finding the creature that roamed the forest?"

"They're not looking for the Beast creature, Adam. They're looking at an ancient Indian ground in the polar regions."

Norland stood quietly. Thinking to himself before answering

back.

"Ancient Indian ground?"

"Said there was some sort of power up there that they've been tracing for a few months now. They went up there to check it out for themselves."

"Does anyone else know about this?"

"No one but me. He only told me of the plan."

"Why you? Why did he keep it secret from everyone else here? He kept it a secret from the team. From me. Who else could he have not told?"

"It's a secret because Nader knows what the power source is."

"Do you know what it is?"

"I do. That's why I warned him not to lead a team of novice agents up there to confront it. Because that power source will kill them without any hesitation or thought."

Up in the polar regions of northern Canada at an ancient Indian ground, Colonel Nader walked through the rough snowy grounds and broken-down trees along with the agents. They searched the area, not finding anything. Nader looked around the snow.

"Find anything?" Nader said.

"No sir."

"It's here. It has to be here."

The snow in front of them begins to glow a bluish hue. Nader looked and pointed over toward the snow.

"Over there! Search over there!"

The agents ran over to the snow, seeing the blue glow from underneath. The agents looked and turned to Nader. Who in turn handed a shovel to one agent that walked over to the other agents.

"Dig it up."

The agents started to dig up the snow with the shovel. They

dug and dug while Nader stood by and watched. The blue glow enlarged itself as the snow began to be removed from the site. After the snow was moved over and dug through, the agents found a Indian burial ground. The looked at it, trying to decipher it. Nader looked and read the inscription that was written on the aged stone.

"We've entered the grounds of the Inuit."

The blue glow turned red and an explosion erupted from the burial site, kicking the agents back and kicking snow up high in the air. Nader crouched behind a tree, looking back at the site. The agents stood up and looked while the snow was falling from the sky, they noticed a figure hovering above the site.

"What is that?" An agent asked

The snow fell and the figure's eyes shined red and raised its arms up toward the agents and released a series of red lightning bolts. Shocking and killing the agents around the site. The agents had burned to death from internal frostbite from the lightning bolts. The remaining snow fell to the ground and Nader peeked to see what happened and his eyes were gazed and locked on the figure that killed the agents. He was in fear of the figure's presence and witness it fly up in the air at shockwave speed, vanishing.

II

<u>COVERED IN DARKNESS</u>

Inside the T.I.T.A.N. Headquarters, Norland searched the office of Nader to try and understand what he went searching for in the Indian grounds in the polar regions. He searched the top of Nader's desk and the desk drawers. Finding nothing that would refer any information about the Indian grounds. Woody entered the office doors and seen Norland searching through the office.

"Something you're looking for boss?"

"Can't find anything that centers on the Indian ground mission."

"You might have to put it to the side for just a quick second."

"Why? We got another mission?"

"Yes sir. One of Suk's laboratories have been picked up by some of T.I.T.A.N.'s outside agents. They want us to head over there and search the place. Possibly find any new clues detailing Suk's previous plots with Kozlov and ADDER."

Norland nodded.

"I'll be right out there."

"Yes sir."

Woody left the office while Norland stated to clean up the office.

Outside in the lobby area of the headquarters, General Sarge Hunter was briefing Whiplash, Nixon, and Woody. Norland had arrived from around the corner. They looked at him. Norland saluted Hunter.

"Commander, I have to say what you all done out there was incredible."

"We were only doing the mission we were given, sir. What is the next one you have for us?"

Hunter commanded them to follow him into his office around the sets of offices nearby. Inside the office, Hunter reached over to his desk and grabbed a remote. He pressed the button toward the board and the board lit up, showing a map of some foreign landmass.

On the landmass was seen a large building, uninhabited and secluded from cities and counties.

"We have this mission for the four of you. This laboratory is one of the few labs that belonged to Kong Suk. Since you brought the bastard in, we need you to head over there to check and see if anything valuable has been left behind."

"You want us to bring back the valuables if we tend to find them?"

"Yes, Commander. Bring them back in one piece. If you are able to find them."

Nixon looked at the landmass very carefully. His mind flowing through his thoughts, memories of previous lands he has stepped foot on. He pointed to the board.

"I know that land."

"I'm sure you do, Nixon. Because that land is here in Canada. In the eastern section of course. Above Quebec."

"We won't let you down, sir." said Norland.

"I am aware you'll get the job done."

Norland and the team prepare themselves with their weapons and gear. The hoverjet sat in the front of the headquarters, ready to take off into the air. Out of the headquarters' doors walk out Norland and the team. They walked toward the jet and entered it as the ramp came down. Inside the jet, Norland walked over to the pilot.

"You were given the orders of the location?"

"Yes, Commander." said the pilot. "Thanks for the heads up."

"No problem."

Norland sat down as the team placed their heavier weapons down in the cabinets and seat holders. He looked at them closely while the ramp slowly closed.

"What do you think we'll find out there, Commander?" Nixon said.

"Whatever has been left behind."

"You don't think Suk had some form of security control over his labs?" Whiplash said. "It would seem like a possibility with a man like him."

"Best we are prepared for everything, Andrea."

"We're about to take off." Woody said. "Hold on guys!"

The hoverjet engines roared as it started to gain speed on the runway. The jet moved faster and faster and it slowly hovered off the ground and flew up into the air. While in the air, Norland looked out of the window down at the headquarters and caught a black jeep driving into the front. Thinking to himself###

"Must be Nader."

Down at the headquarters, Nader exited out of the jeep, running inside the headquarters with panic on his face. Nader bolted through the doors and stood in the middle of the lobby area.

"I need everyone's attention right now!" Nader said. "Listen to me very, very carefully!"

Everyone inside the building stood quiet and surrounded

Nader. Listening closely to what he is about to tell them. Uncertain and unaware of what the actions of his words will be and what they concern.

"We have a problem. A threatening problem and I need all of you agents to be on high alert. The project that myself and the agents went on were drastically wrong. The agents were killed, and I am the only one that escaped to come here and tell all of you here, something ancient has risen."

"What kind of ancient if we may know, sir?" an agent said.

"I will tell you more about it later. Right now, I need all of you to get to your communication devices and contacts all satellite controllers to tell them to search for a high level of energy around the northern parts of Canada. That way, we can find it faster before it kills anyone else."

Nader walked away and standing in front of him was Flm. Nader calmed down a bit and nodded to Flm.

"We need to talk."

"I agree with you."

Nader walked with Flm into his laboratory and closed the door. Flm sat down at his table while Nader walked toward him and sat in the neighboring chair. Flm could see the fear on Nader's face.

"Did you find what you went looking for?" Flm said. "Because the way you're looking right now, you seem to have found him."

"We did and he killed all of the agents in one shot. He raised his hands up and these red lightning bolts jolted from his hands and went right through the agents, burning them from the inside."

"Did they look as if they were going through immediate frostbite?"

"That's exactly how they appeared. I couldn't do anything to help them."

"The man you saw. Was he wearing a black uniform with

ancient markings on it?"

Nader sat and thought, for a few seconds of thinking, he looked at Flm.

"Yes. He did. Some kind of Indian markings were on his uniform."

Flm nodded.

"Just as I suspected it to be."

"What did you suspect?"

"I know who the man is and why he has risen from the Indian grounds."

"Well, who was that man. That warrior who killed my agents in a quick second?"

"He is known throughout the native lands as one of their ancient gods. Primarily his name escapes me, but they were known to call him the Black Sector."

"The Black Sector?"

"His history is surrounded with dread and destruction. Indian mythology tends to say he was once a mortal man who was chosen by a higher force and was granted powers beyond human belief. With those powers, he was charged to use them for the good of his people and apparently, he did. It wasn't until the death of his wife and son that he began to use those powers for evil and revenge. That revenge in his spirit is what banished him into the depths of the earth. Now, you've seemed to have awoken him and now he's still out for the revenge he once sought out."

Nader exhaled slowly and stood up from the seat. He nodded and shook Flm's hand.

"I have to thank you for your extensive knowledge of all this kind of stuff. No one else here knows about this but the two of us."

"Norland knows about the Indian grounds."

"Does he know about the Black Sector?"

"He does not. Not yet anyway."

"Make sure it stays that way until it's time for him to know."

"Yes sir. I will do so."

"Where is Norland now?"

"He and the team have been sent on a mission to one of Suk's secluded laboratories. They should be back after they have completed the searching of the place."

Nader nodded.

"Once again, I thank you for your loyalty and trust, Professor Flm."

Nader walked out of the laboratory and closed the door behind him. Flm sat at his desk, thinking to himself while counting.

The hoverjet flew over a set of trees before seeing the secluded laboratory. The laboratory was covered in snow and downed branches from the nearby trees. Norland looked out of the window toward the lab.

"Think you can land down here?"

"I know I can, Commander." the pilot said. "Won't be a problem for me."

Norland smiled and walked toward the team, who were preparing themselves for the landing of the jet.

"Now, when we go inside the lab, we look for whatever is valuable to take back to the headquarters and we leave in one piece. Can we do that?"

"We can, Commander." Nixon said. "No problems from us."

Norland nodded.

"Very well then, let's do this task."

The hoverjet landed in front of the laboratory. The ramp came down and out came Norland and the team. They stood in front of the lab, searching and gazing at its surroundings. Whiplash looked at how close the lab was to the forest.

"You think any animals are living inside right now?"

"That is a possibility." Norland said. "We need to heighten our guard more so."

Norland looked at the lab doors. He pointed toward them as the team looked onward at the doors.

"We head in, search for what we can find, and we leave. A simple plan for this."

"Yeah." Hawk said. "We probably won't have to fight any of Suk's soldiers or any ADDER agents."

"We can only hope."

They ran toward the laboratory doors. Once in front of the doors, Norland gave to the count of three and kicked in the doors. Inside the lab was hardly anything but left behind equipment and tables. The lab was cold, chilly, and damp. There was even some snow that made its way inside the lab from the holes in the ceiling and windows. The floor was wet from the melting snow.

"It's cold in here." Hawk mentioned with a shiver.

"Keep your guard up, Woody." Norland said. "Don't let it down because of a temperature change."

They walked through the cold lab, searching every room they came up on. Finding nothing but old equipment and left behind documents on laboratory structuring. Nixon looked around and walked toward Norland.

"Appears this lab was cleaned out before Suk abandoned it."

"Seems to be the case, Steve."

Hawk and Whiplash approached Norland and Nixon. Neither have they found anything valuable themselves. Norland nodded.

"Very well. Let's return to the headquarters. Tell them this place was a dud."

They prepared to leave and while walking towards the door, Hawk is pulled back and slammed to the ground by an unseen force. Norland turned around seeing Hawk on the ground. Nixon pulled out his guns and Whiplash released her electric whips.

Norland helped Hawk to his feet.

"What happened to you?"

"I…. I don't have any idea. Felt like someone pulled me back and knocked me to the ground."

"But there's no one behind you." Nixon said. "How would that even be a possibility to consider."

They stood quiet and heard what sounded like footsteps around them. The footsteps began to increase as if someone was running. The footsteps inched closer to them and Nixon was shoved to the wall, Whiplash was hit in the stomach and knocked to the ground, and Hawk was slammed to the ground from behind again. Norland stood his ground, circling his position and heard the footsteps.

"We're fighting ghosts now." Norland gestured. "Because I don't recall ghosts being a threat to us."

The footsteps stopped in front of Norland and the invisible figure began to form a shape. The figure uncloaked itself and revealed itself to Norland. He looked and recognized the suit the figure wore.

"Where did you acquire the cloaking armor?"

"From Suk and ADDER of course." said the figure. "They hired me to watch over all of their locations. Including this lab here."

"Who are you?"

"My name is Harvey Madison. But you and your weak team can call me the Spyghost."

"Well, Spyghost. I am Commander Norland, and this is my team. We were here to search for anything needed of T.I.T.A.N. But since you're here and you made the first hit, we're here to take you out."

The team stood up and seen the Spyghost. They prepared themselves for the coming fight.

"Sure. If you can catch me in the clearness."

The Spyghost pressed a button on his wrist and cloaked into the shadows. Unseen from Norland and the team. Norland and the team form a close circle. Covering each other's backs and having a clear vision of their surroundings.

"Watch yourselves." Norland said. "He can be anywhere."

They circled their location and heard the footsteps of the Spyghost coming toward them. Norland could recognize the footsteps were behind him, meaning in the eyesight of Nixon.

"Nixon, he's heading for you."

"I got him."

"We will see about that, boy!" Spyghost said.

The Spyghost uncloaked and went for a punch toward Nixon. Nixon grabbed his arm and threw him against the wall. Nixon started firing shots at Spyghost, though he kicked the gun out of Nixon's hands and elbowed him in the face. Whiplash grabbed him with her electric whips. Spyghost looked at her and glanced at the whips. He smiled through his mask.

"Why would you choose whips as your choice of weaponry. Tempting to answer I see."

Spyghost grabbed her whips and pulled her closer to him to where he head-butted her in the face, knocking her out. Nixon grabbed him from behind, but Spyghost pulled him over his shoulder, slamming him on the ground and kicked him in his face. Hawk rammed Spyghost through one of the laboratory doors with his shield. Spyghost started pounding Hawk in his back with his arms, pushing him down to the ground. Spyghost kicked Hawk in the face and grabbed his shield.

"I like your shield. You don't mind if I keep it after I decapitate you with it?"

Spyghost raised the shield above his head and Norland ran into the lab, spearing Spyghost against the lab tables and desk behind him. Norland started punching Spyghost in the abdomen and slammed him atop the table. Spyghost kicked Norland in the face and hit him in the head with a chair. Norland shook off the attack and grabbed Ghost man by his head and slammed him against the desk and kicked him through the lab door.

"This one is strong. Very strong."

"I am strong. You are fast." Norland said.

"A great fight in the making."

Spyghost ran toward Norland, but Norland snatched him by his head, elbowed him in the face and slammed him to the floor.

"This is over, Harvey."

"Not until I am completely unconscious or dead."

Spyghost pressed the cloaking button on his wrist and Norland extended his hand and out flew a blue lightning bolt, which struck Spyghost's wrist, breaking the cloaking device. Spyghost looked and started beating the cloaking device with his fist.

"What was that?!"

"That was my hidden strength."

Norland ran toward Spyghost and hit him in the head with an uppercut. The force of the uppercut knocked Spyghost down and unconscious. Spyghost is defeated as the team is recovering. Norland walked over to them each, asking if they were alright. They stated they were. Norland grabbed Hawk's shield and handed it back to him.

"Thanks for the save, Commander." Hawk said.

"We're a team. We protect each other."

Nixon looked at the unconscious body of Spyghost. He walked over and pulled out his gun, placing it onto Spyghost's head. Norland sees it and ran toward him.

"I'm going to put this fool out of his misery."

"No, you're not, Steve."

"Why not. He's an enemy. We have to eliminate him."

"We're not going to eliminate him. We're taking him back with us to the headquarters. He can't cloak. I took out his cloaking device.”

Nixon placed his gun back into its holster as Norland kneeled down and grabbed Spyghost. He looked at Nixon.

“Give me a hand.”

Nixon hesitantly help hold up Spyghost as they were leaving the laboratory. While leaving, the ground began to shake, and the laboratory ceiling collapsed atop them. Norland looked through the falling debris and the dust in the air for the team.

“Are you ok?!” Norland said. “Someone answer me!”

Norland caught a figure standing in the dust and debris. A large figure. Almost a physical match for Norland. He looked and realized that the figure wasn’t one of the team members nor was it Spyghost.

“Who are you?” Norland said.

“I sense his power surging within you.” The figure said. “Allow me to siphon it from you.”

The dust cleared and Norland found himself staring in the eyes of the Black Sector.

III

<u>AN ANCIENT CAUSE</u>

The Black Sector stared down Norland while the team was buried underneath the debris of the laboratory's ceiling. His eyes were locked onto Norland, sensing the power surging from him. Norland stood up as much as he could from the previous fight with Spyghost and the collapse of the laboratory's ceiling.

"He chose you to be my successor." Sector said. "I disagree with his choosing."

"What are you talking about?" said Norland. "Successor of what?"

"No more reasons to talk to you. I have risen from my seclusion to kill you in order to grant my revenge from those who murdered my family."

Nixon, Hawk, and Whiplash slowly came up from the debris and looked at Norland. Seeing him staring at Black Sector, they prepared themselves for the fight that was coming. Sector glanced at the team and smirked.

"Who the hell is that guy?" Hawk asked.

"You three believe you're on par with this man?! He is beyond your capabilities. The three of you combined couldn't withstand his power. If he was smart on how to use it in this world."

"How about you try to take us on yourself." Nixon said. "See what kind of man you are to us. See if you can match our

116

Commander's strength."

Sector nodded and set his arms down.

"I will do what I must."

Sector flew toward Nixon and shoulder tackled him against the wall. Whiplash used her whips to grab Sector by his arms. She held on to Sector's struggling as much as she could, but it wasn't successful as sector grabs the whips and snapped them from her arms and punched her into the ground. Hawk ran toward Sector and attempted to beat him down with his shield. Sector laughed at the coming attacks.

"What kind of warriors are you?"

Sector grabbed the shield and punched right through it, cracking the shield. Hawk, shocked and in a state of confusion fell to the ground, looking at his broke shield. Sector grabbed him and threw him against Nixon at the wall.

Sector smiled and turned toward Norland.

"You should be a more worthy opponent. A true warrior."

"I will fight until my last breath."

"If that is your true purpose, I consider you take an inhale and slowly exhale at this very moment. For your last few seconds are among you."

Sector lunged at Norland and attacked him with a series of punches. The punches harmed Norland as Sector kicked Norland across the hallway, falling into the debris on the ground.

"He couldn't have chosen you. YOU! You're not even fighting back!"

"Just wait and see what I can do."

"I am here. So why should I wait. Fight me, boy!"

Norland stood up, seeing Sector in the air coming down in front of him with his fist. Norland jumped up with his fist in the air and the two collided. The intensity of the collision shook the laboratory, thus causing the place to collapse and fall apart. Norland looked and seen the building falling. He turned and

Sector punched him in the face, knocking him out. Sector looked around and started laughing.

"I will take out my vengeance on these people of today. Since they're the children of those that killed my people. I will kill them. A just act in progress."

Sector levitated in the air above Norland and the team. Sector looked down at Norland, who in turn had gazed up toward Sector.

"When you have the strength in you, find me. I'll be at your most crowded city that there is around these lands."

Sector flew off like a bolt. Norland grabbed his partners and escaped the falling laboratory. They made it outside just as the laboratory fell to the ground. The pilot walked out of the hoverjet toward Norland, seeing how he and the team are tired and beaten.

"What happened in there, Commander?"

"Blind assault is what happened. Take us back to headquarters, please."

"Yes sir."

They entered the jet and flew away from the site, returning to the headquarters. Inside the jet, the entire team is tired. None are speaking nor are they hardly moving. Norland sat by himself, mediating on who Black Sector is and what the words had meant concerning him as some kind of successor.

"What did he mean?" Norland said to himself. "What was he talking about? Successor? Successor of what is the question?"

They returned to the headquarters with agents assisting the team inside the building. Norland is fully rested as the rest of the team were still dealing with their loss and pain in the laboratory. Norland looked at them, seeing them exhausted.

"Make sure they're taken care of." Norland said to an agent.

"I will, Commander."

Norland looked around and spotted Hunter speaking with Nader. He walked over toward them quickly. Hunter and Nader looked, seeing Norland approaching them. Nader is prepared for what Norland will say or do.

"Commander, whatever you have to say or do just do it."

"Can I have a word in private with you, Colonel?"

"Of course."

Norland followed Nader into his office and Nader closed the office doors as Norland stood in the middle of the office full of tension and concern about his place in the team.

"I know you're going to ask me about the Indian grounds."

"I am. I want to know why it was kept a secret from us and why did you even bother to mess with it. You know the lore of Indian grounds."

"I do. I also know the power they seem to possess and gather over the centuries. That kind of power is what this world sorely needs."

"Power like the man myself and the team ran into? That man, full of power and strength. I couldn't even take him, let alone the entire team. You woke him up from his hibernation and now he intends on destroying whatever he sees as a threat to him and his cause."

"The man you saw is called The Black Sector. He's an ancient figure. Supposedly from Indian mythology."

"So, you've basically woke up a god."

"He's not a god. He's a superhuman being. Possesses power far more than most humans can imagine. Simply put, if any humans has possessed his power, they would ultimately fall victim to it with only a few that would survive it within them."

"He said that I was his successor. I don't know what that meant. I'm still trying to figure that out."

Nader stared at Norland for a bit. He later nodded and knew what to do.

"Go see Professor Flm. He will have the answer to that question."

"I was just about to see him."

Norland walked out of the office, leaving Nader inside who sat at his desk, looking out of the window into the forest ahead.

Norland walked down the hallway and knocked on Flm's laboratory door.

"Come in." said Flm.

Norland entered the laboratory and Flm spotted him immediately. He stood up from his chair to greet Norland.

"Adam, good to see you again. I saw how the team looked when you came in. What happened out there?"

"We were ambushed by a guy named Harvey Madison. Called himself the Spyghost. We dealt with him and brought him along with us. He should be in a cell right now. We were also attacked by the Black Sector. That's why I came to talk with you."

"What did the Black Sector say?"

"He said that I was his successor. That I was chosen.'

Flm nodded.

"I knew this would come about at this particular time. Though the time is right for it."

"About what?"

"The day you were granted your power. The figure you said you saw give it to you. He is the same figure that granted Sector his power and ability."

"I'm not seeing where all of this is going."

"Let me explain. The figure you seen in your near-death experience on the battlefield is the same figure that made Sector who he is today. The figure you saw, the man you saw that day is known throughout the legends as Lord Blizzard. He is the one who chose Sector in the past and he is the one that has chosen you."

"Chose me for what purpose? To be Sector's successor?"

"Yes. Sector started out using his power for good. It wasn't until he lost his family that he turned to evil and from what is known throughout history, Blizzard wasn't pleased of Sector's turn. So, it seems to me that he chose you to take Sector's place in this universe. You have a better and stronger heart than Sector ever will. I've told you before, your power isn't a curse. It's a blessing in disguise."

Norland nodded.

"I seem to understand what you're saying. Though it is still hard for me to accept."

"You have a choice to make this day, Adam. Either you can choose to accept that your power is a curse and allow Sector to hunt you down and kill you. Plus destroy the world as we know it or you can fully accept your power as a blessing and defeat Sector. Proving to him and Blizzard that you are his successor."

"I understand you."

"I hope you do."

They hear noise and raked motions coming from outside the laboratory. They get up and walked to the door. Norland opened the door and from the hallway ran Suk, escaped from his prison cell. He laughed as he ran through the building with agents chasing him.

"This is my time!" Suk said. "I have escaped a T.I.T.A.N. prison and facility!"

Norland ran out toward Suk and speared him into the wall and threw him on the ground. Suk looked and seen Norland standing over him with his foot placed on his throat.

"You're going back to your cell, Suk."

"I will have my day, Canadian. You can assure yourself on that."

The agents arrived and surrounded Suk. They picked him up and placed him in handcuffs, walking him back down the hallway toward his cell block. Norland turned back to Flm at the lab door.

"I will take some time to think on all of this."

"You should and I know deep down that you'll make the right decision, Adam."

Norland shook Flm's hand and left the lab door.

Somewhere in the air, flies Black Sector. He hovered in the air, searching the land around him. He gazed and looked, seeing only forests and country lands. He keened his eyes forward and noticed a set of buildings in the far distance. The city was further away than it appeared to look. He thought for a minute.

"Appears to be a city far ahead. A large one."

Sector flew toward that city. He passed by a street sign that read Grimsby - 8, Hamilton - 31, and Toronto - 89. The city that Sector keen his eyes on in the far distance was indeed Toronto.

Inside the headquarters, Norland sat in his room alone. He sat quietly and mediated for almost three hours nonstop. He sat and mediated, thinking of what Flm had told him about Lord Blizzard and Black Sector. He sat still and instantly began to feel a chill in the room. He opened his eyes and looked around. Finding himself no longer in his room, but in a snow filled place. The ground was covered in snow and snow was continually falling from the sky. The sun shined down on the place, but the sun wasn't strong enough to melt all the snow that laid on the ground.

Norland looked in the distance and seen a throne. He ran over to the throne and seen the chair, also someone sitting inside the chair. He ran toward them and seen the size of the man that sat in the throne. Hesitated, Norland slowly approached him, but the man was already aware of Norland's presence.

"I know you're here. You don't have to be afraid of me Adam Watson of Canada."

Norland stopped walking slow and stood facing the man.

"Who are you and what is this place?"

"This place is my realm. A realm of snow and ice for all eternity. Though until time has ended of course."

"Are you who Flm told me about?"

"I am the Lord Blizzard. I am an ancient presence that has lived on through countless eons. I have chosen many to be soldiers of the cold. Many of them had waxed cold and only a few remained with a heart of flesh. You, Watson, possess a heart of flesh."

"Are you some kind of god?"

"I am no god. There is only one true god. I was created by Him to watch over the snow and ice until the time was appointed where it needed to be rained down upon the earth. Until then, I sit here and wait patiently. I also picked those who are worthy to be my heralds."

"You chose me?"

"I did choose you. You are the successor to those that failed me in the past. You are the successor of the Black Sector."

"I had a confrontation with him. He is determined to exact his revenge on the people that wronged him and killed his family."

"As he has always been. I can understand his revenge, but he takes it out on those that are not even a part of the people that killed his wife and son and destroyed his land. He could not see it any other way. He has made his choice and that is why you must defeat him. To put an end to his rage once and for all."

"He's very powerful. I'm not sure if I can take him down."

"You can defeat him. You have the same exact power he possesses. It only depends on how open your heart is to the universe and to yourself. If you can believe you can defeat him by faith, then you possess the power to defeat him."

Blizzard looked up in the air as he eyes turned a solid blue. Norland looked up and witnessed heavy snow falling form the sky.

"Your time here in this realm is up Adam Watson of Canada."

"Wait! I still have more to ask you!"

"Ask me another time. You have business to fulfill in your world. Fulfill it you must."

The heavy snow fell on Norland, enclosing him inside the snow as he tried to crawl out of it. The snow built up on him to the point where he couldn't breathe. Instantly, Norland awoke inside his room at the headquarters. Catching his breath, he has made up his mind and stands up from the floor and approached his closet. Gathering his uniform and equipment.

In the lobby, the team sat alongside other agents, talking about the laboratory event and Black sector. From the hallway, Norland walked out with a new uniform, covered with the colors of white and red. He nodded at his team and prepared to exit the building. Once outside, Nader came from behind him and stopped him.

"Where are you going, Commander?"

"Black Sector is headed for Toronto. I intend on confronting him and stopping him before he kills any innocent people."

"You're going alone on this one?"

"I have to. This is between myself and Sector. Goes far beyond human reasoning."

From the headquarter doors come the team, still in pain. Woody walked over to Norland.

"You sure you don't need us to aid you in this?"

"I'll be fine. Take care of yourselves first. Worry about me later."

"Yes sir."

Woody stepped back alongside Nixon and Andrea. They watched Norland enter a hoverjet on his own. He turned on the engine, preparing to take off. He drove the jet down the runway and lifted it up into the air, flying away from the eyesight of the team. Heading for Toronto.

From the window, Flm watched the jet disappear into the sky. He turned back to his table and let out a small smile.

"He has chosen his decision."

IV

A DARK SECTOR

The city of Toronto is in utter chaos as Black Sector had arrived and is destroying everything, he gazes his eyes on. The civilians run in horror, in mass trying to escape the city. Traffic jammed in the streets with some leaving their vehicles behind in order to save themselves from Sector's lightning blasts. In the air only a few miles away is Norland in the hoverjet. In the distance he can see the smoke and flames coming from the city.

"He's already there."

The hoverjet increased its speed, moving faster in the air toward Toronto. In the city, Sector began to grab nearby civilians and torture them with electric bolts into their bodies. Killing them in the same manner as the agents in the polar regions of the Indian grounds. Civilians scream in horror as they are dying to death from internal frostbite by Sector's lightning bolts.

"Where is your savior of today?!" Sector asked. "Who will come to protect all of you from me? I sense no one! You are all alone! Left to your own devices and thinking patterns to save yourselves. Such a weak generation of Man."

Sector can hear the sound of engines in the air and he glanced up, seeing the hoverjet above him. He looked at the cockpit and seen Norland. Sector's eyes lit up with enthusiasm and excitement.

"Ah. Finally. He has grown a pair."

The hoverjet landed directly in the downtown streets of Toronto. Civilians run past the jet as Norland stared at Sector from the cockpit. Sector stood on the street with his arms open, waiting for Norland to exit the jet and face him.

"Come! Come, successor. Face me like a man!"

"If that is what you wish."

Norland shut down the jet and the ramp came down. Sector couldn't wait for Norland to exit the jet and approach him. Coming down the ramp is Norland slowly, wearing a helmet of his own in the style of his uniform. Sector began to get impatient with waiting.

"Hurry it up, boy!"

Norland stepped foot on the street, he walked away from the jet into the open street, facing Sector.

"Finally! You have prepared yourself for death I see."

"I didn't come here to die, Sector. I came to prove to you that I am here to take your place."

"My place. You seek my place? You'll never earn it, boy!"

"I won't have to earn it. I'm going to take it."

"Is that right? Come on then, boy. Take my place."

"As you command."

Norland ran toward Sector and dropkicked him. The dropkick was intense that he pushed Sector into a set of cars behind him. Sector looked and stared at Norland. Norland stood in the street, gesturing Sector to come and fight him. Sector laughed.

"He's got the strength in him. Finally, a real fight against a real warrior."

Sector jolted from the cars and rammed into Norland, knocking him across the street and into a nearby building. Inside the building, Norland stood up and spotted a set of civilians hiding inside the building. They stared at Norland and looked out at Sector and turned back to Norland.

"Get out of here!" Norland yelled. "Go now!"

As the civilians were fleeing the building, Sector flew into the building and grabbed Norland by his neck and slammed him into a table that sat nearby. He started to kick Norland in the gut and increased his strength. He kicked Norland out of the building and out onto the street.

"Show me your true strength, boy!" Sector said. "I demand a real fight with you."

"Don't worry yourself, Sector." Norland said. "You're going to get a real fight. A brutal one indeed."

"Well, bring it to me!"

Norland ran toward the flying Sector. Both of their fists out in front. The two collide fist to fist, creating a shockwave, knocking out the windows of the nearby buildings and pushing one another across the city in opposite directions. The city is being destroyed by the two adversaries. Sector looked around himself, seeing nothing but debris of buildings and cars and dead civilians. He looked out in the distance, seeing Norland standing up from the impact of the shockwave.

"You are strong, boy! What else do you possess in that body of yours that came from him?"

Norland looked at Sector.

"More than enough to defeat you here and now."

Sector flew toward Norland, who was already running toward him. The two collide fighting each other nonstop. Throwing punches and kicks at one another. Knocking each other into buildings and slamming themselves into the pavement, causing large holes in the streets. Sector kicked Norland in the head and punched him in the back. Norland fell to his knees as Sector kicked him in the face.

"You seem to be getting tired." Sector said. "You should've prepared for this moment, boy! I've been waiting centuries for this!"

"I'm still here and I'm still breathing." Norland said. "I can do this all day if we have to."

Sector laughed.

"We don't have all day. I don't have all day to deal with you. I plan on killing you, then killing these weak vessels. Then I will attack all of your cities and rid this world of the weakness that dwells inside of it and above it. After the destruction is completed, I will be this world's new savior!"

"Not until I am dead and laying in my grave."

"Don't ask for it so early, boy! I have a place prepared just for you anyhow."

"I didn't ask for it. I'm stating it."

Norland raised up and punched Sector in the face and kicked him in the legs, knocking him to his knees. Norland stood back and delivered an uppercut to Sector, knocking him to the ground. Sector doesn't move for a bit as Norland took the time to regain his breath and strength.

"You are one of the toughest men I have fought in my life." Norland said.

As Norland was taking his breath, Sector rose up and snatched Norland by the throat. Laughing maniacally in his face.

"One of you say?!" Sector said. "I am the only one you have ever faced with this feat of strength! There is no other!"

Sector stood up and held Norland up above him, choking him. Norland tried to kicked Sector, but the kicks weren't having any kind of effect on Sector. Norland thought to himself that it seemed Sector had an increase of strength and energy, making him stronger than before.

"Your kicks won't have an effect on me!" Sector mocked. "I am stronger than you can imagine! And he chose you of all the people on this earth to be my successor? How weak he has become to do such a task. A waste of life he chooses in a desperate waste of shame."

"He chose me because I am a better man than you'll ever be,

Sector. I am more proven to do the task necessary and use the power for good rather than for vengeance against those who wronged me. I would've dealt with them sooner and with a just heart and mind."

Sector slammed Norland to the ground and raised him up again. Never letting go of Norland's throat during the continuous slamming.

"You weren't there in those days when those foreigners came and took our land! They killed our wives and our children. The killed most of the strong men and left the weak ones alive. I fought for my people and I almost died in the process. But, the Blizzard Lord sought me out and seen something in me that was different than the rest. Strength and might. With that, he gave me this power and I thought, since he gave it to me, I have the right to do with it as I wish. To do with it what is right in my own eyes."

"That is your problem? You seek to use it only for yourself and not those in need."

"I aided those that needed help and assistance. I received no thanks in return from them and they went about their business as if nothing ever happened. I wasn't going to take that as a thank you or an appreciation for my help. So, I killed them. Every last one of them."

"Because of your selfishness and folly."

"NO!"

Sector slammed Norland into the pavement with a stronger force and slammed him against a nearby truck. Choking him more so than before with Norland struggling to breathe.

"They didn't lose a wife! They didn't lose a son! I did! I decided to show them what it was like to lose that was is closest to you and they felt it. The same feeling I received when I saw my wife and son dead at my feet by those foreigners."

"You know what your weakness is Sector? It's your rage. It

blinds you from seeing who you really are. You can't see what you're doing at this very moment. Your rage is controlling you. Something that you lack is willpower. You're letting the past dictate to you your future. Your wife is gone. Your son is gone. Your people are gone. You can change all of that if you stop being a selfish man with a vengeance."

"I will not tolerate this nonsense!"

Sector tossed Norland into a building and flew up in the air, slamming onto Norland's body. Norland screamed from the pain he felt as Sector grabbed Norland head and removed his helmet, throwing it down the street. Sector stomped on Norland's neck.

"Your end has come, boy! I hope you're prepared for the other side."

"I hope you're prepared for what is about to come."

"Which is what?"

"A side-attack."

Sector looked around at the city and gazed back at Norland.

"What side attack?"

Sector turned around and was ambushed by Hawk, Nixon, and Whiplash from an incoming hoverjet. Norland smiled as he seen his team come in and they're taking the fight to Sector. Hawk required a new shield made up of solidium, Whiplash reverie a new set of whips made of kinetillucium-laced fabrics, and Nixon has prepared himself with a sleek body armor that gives him enhanced strength. Sector looked at the team, seeing Norland stand up on his feet in front of them. Norland glanced at his team and pointed to Sector.

"Let's take him out!"

Sector flew toward them and punched Hawk, but his solidium shield held against the attack. Sector noticed his punch didn't dent or break the shield.

"What is that made of?"

"A mineral that you can find at your local Avago Land shop."

Hawk said.

He rammed the shield into the face of Sector, knocking him back. Whiplash grabbed him with her whips. He noticed them and scoffed.

"Again, with these!"

He grabbed the whips and jolted them with his lightning bolts. The lighting covered the whips and suddenly the whips absorbed the lightning bolts. Sector was appalled.

"No one has been able to withstand my power!"

"You can thank the kinetillucium for that, Mr. Sector." Whiplash said as she tossed him into a building with the whips.

"I can get this one hit on him." Nixon said. "Trust me, it will be worth watching."

Nixon ran toward Sector, who stood up from the building hit. Nixon punched Sector with his armor enhancing his strength. The armor increased his strength to the point that the punch slammed Sector into the ground, causing a small crater.

Nixon turned to Norland, smiling.

"He's all yours to finish off, Commander."

"Let me do so." Norland said.

Norland approached Sector, who was laying on the ground, near beaten from the team's upgraded attacks. Sector looked into Norland's eyes and started to laugh.

"What are you waiting for, boy?" Sector said. "Finish me off. Kill me."

"I'm not going to kill you."

"You're weak. You'll always be weak."

"I'm going to show you why I am your successor and replacement."

Norland raised his head and glanced up toward the sky. Small snippets of snow started to fall from the sky onto the city. Norland's eyes lit of a light blue. He found himself levitating into the air. The team watched on, uncertain of what to make of the event they were witnessing. Norland turned his attention on Sector, staring at him with the glowing blue eyes.

"What are you doing?" Sector said. "I've never seen this before."

"Because I have surpassed you."

Norland glanced up and a blue lightning bolt came crashing down on Sector. The bolt electrocuted him and started freezing him in a set of ice. The bolt disappeared leaving on Sector shocked and sealed in ice. Norland levitated onto the ground as the team approached him.

"What was that?" Hawk said.

"It was his power." Nixon said. "His real power."

Norland and the team restore Toronto as they take Sector back to the headquarters with them and they leave in their hover jets

After two weeks, Sector has been sent to a secure prison on the outskirts of North America and the team is back in actions in doing missions across the world, searching for any remaining traces of ADDER. Norland walked into the headquarters, prepared for his next mission. He approached the receptionist who called out to him.

"Yes ma'am" Norland said.

"You have a visitor in your room."

Norland stood quiet.

"A visitor?"

"Yes."

Norland nodded.

"Thank you for telling me."

Norland walked down the hallway and entered his room. Inside his room stood Nathan Hawke. He seen Norland and smiled.

"Hi." Hawke said.

"Hi to you too." Norland said as he shut the door.

"I know this is unusual for you to see me here. In your room. At this place."

"Why are you here?"

"I'm sure you know who I am, correct?"

"I know who you are. Nathan Hawke, CEO of Hawke Industries. I also know that you're the Nano Man."

Hawke scoffed.

"You know your people I see."

"I know the ones I need to know about."

"Fair enough. I am here because I have a proposition for you. Something that Nader has been doing for a while now and the time has come to present it to you."

"What is it? A mission?

"Yeah, it's a mission all right."

"What kind of mission is this? I would assume it's important if Nader sent you to deliver it to me."

"It's a planetary concern."

"How concerning is it?"

"If we don't stop what's coming, we won't have a world to live in. That's how important this is."

Norland nodded.

"So, when do we begin."

THE UNSTOPPABLE BEAST BEING HUNTED

I

ON THE HUNT

In the northern Canadian forests, the United States Military continues their search for Kent Brock under the orders of General Lawler. The soldiers continue the search, finding nothing but torn clothing fragments and little sprinkles of blood in the snow.

"Is this where he was last spotted by the last patrol group?" A soldier asked.

"Yes. He was here. Apparently, he killed the last group. Let's hope that we don't make the same mistake."

"We won't."

After hours of searching the forest, being unsuccessful in finding Brock or the Beast in the forest, the military returns to the Canadian base where Lawler waited for them to respond. The military jeeps drive toward the base, Lawler bolted through the base door towards the front jeep.

"Have you found him?" Lawler asked.

"We did not, General." The soldier said. "We can continue to search if you command us."

"We're done up here. He wouldn't still be hiding in the same place as last time. He's probably gone down south. Prepare yourselves and your colleagues to make a return trip to the United States. Kent Brock must be somewhere in the country and in intend to find the fugitive."

The jeeps turned around and drove from the base. Lawler exited the base and entered a jeep of his own. He directed the driver to take him to the aerial base for a helicopter ride into the United States.

In the northern borders of the United States, somewhere in the northern parts of Montana is Kent Brock, running through the woods and found himself on a roadway that lead to a small town. Brock walked down the roadway toward the town. Making it into the town, Brock walked into a small local place and approached the counter, seeing the counter clerk standing and staring at him.

"Sir, looks like you've been through some trouble."

"I prefer not to talk about it. May I use a phone. I don't have one of my own on me."

"I take it you lost it during your trouble."

The clerk looked down at Brock's leg, seeing the gunshot wound. Brock looked and stood still.

"You could say that."

The clerk nodded as she handed him the store phone. He used it to contact a close friend. A friend named James Porter, who lived nearby the small town.

"Come on, James. Pick up. Pick up."

James picked up the line on his side and responded to Brock. Concern about where Brock has been over the past few days and worried about him and his scientific involvement with the government.

"Where have you been, man?" James said. "You wouldn't answer your phone."

"Because I lost it in the woods."

"What were you doing in the woods?"

"I'll explain everything to you if you can come here and pick me up."

"Where are you?"

"I'm in some small town. I'm using a store's phone to speak with you. You don't live very far from here, James."

"I'm on my way, Kent. Just stay where you are."

"Thank you."

Brock ended the call and handed the phone back to the clerk.

"Got yourselves settled?"

"Seems to be the case."

The clerk walked over to the drink section of the store and took a water bottle and gave it to Brock. He stared at her, waiting for her to give him the total price of the water bottle.

"I don't have any money on me, ma'am."

"Don't worry about it. It's on the house. Rom the way you look with your torn clothing, covered in dirt, I felt you needed something with you."

Kent nodded.

"Thank you again."

Brock sat at a table and waited for James to arrive. Approximately after thirty minutes, James pulled up in front of the store with Brock walking outside toward his car. James shook his head as Brock approached the passenger's seat.

"Look at you, man."

"This isn't the worst I've looked."

"You can tell me everything back at the place."

"I will. I'll tell you everything that I went through so you can calm your conscious."

"This isn't funny."

"I know. This is life. Life sometimes takes situations like this and laughs. A humor of its own."

James drove away from the store, leaving the small town and heading out on the roadway, returning to his town and home.

11

GENUINE SOLDIER REQUESTED

Lawler and his small army of soldiers passed through the United States-Canada border, entering the state of Montana. Their jeeps driving through the snow-covered roads, entering the roadway where Brock was previously walking.

Lawler looked down at the snow while a soldier drove the jeep, Lawler noticed human footprints in the snow to the side of the road.

"He's been through here!" Lawler said. "Keep going forward."

"There's a small town up ahead, General." The soldier said. "You want us to enter in?"

"Yes. He may have went there to make some phone call or something with communications. He had to have spoken with someone and we're going to find out who."

"Yes sir."

The jeeps drove down the roadway, toward the small town. Believing that Brock may be still residing there for shelter and safety. Not knowing that he's already left the small town and is heading further south of Montana.

James entered the driveway of his home, which is mostly a cabin-built home in the wilderness. He parked the car in the driveway as Brock got out of the car, walking toward the home door. James exited the car and approached the door, unlocking it, opening the door, allowing Brock to enter the home first.

"I have to thank you again for allowing me into your home, James."

"You have to thank me for a lot of things. No telling if the military already have my address, since they possibly have taken your items and files."

"They didn't take the files. I hid them in a safe place. They won't even come up to them nor see them."

"Well, that's good to hear."

"I figured you would say that. Since some of your stuff was also in the pile."

"No shit, Kent. Those papers of mine could change the foundation of industrialization as we know it. We cannot let the government get their hands on it. No matter what."

"They won't get their hands on it. Trust me, I've taken care of all the possible problems."

James nodded. Kent walked over to the couch and sat down. Seeing James grabbing his phone, dialing down a number.

"Who are you calling?"

"I'm calling Charlotte. Tell her you're up here with me."

"You don't need to bring her into this."

"No, I do. She's been wanting to see you since the

accident. Don't be afraid of her because she's related to the Commando General guy."

"I would see it best if I avoided her at all cost. She could eventually slip and tell him that she knows where I am. Which would bring him here to your doorstep and I'm positive you wouldn't like the government trespassing into your own home."

"They do it to almost everyone now, Kent. We live in a police state."

"I know it firsthand."

"You surely do."

"I'll be in the other room. Get some rest if you can."

"I will do that."

James walked into the other room to speak with Charlotte. Kent laid his head back on the couch, falling asleep. A sleep he thought he would never get the chance to do again after the accident and the manhunt for him by the governments of the world.

Lawler and the army enter the small town, frightening the residents with their jeeps and geared up uniforms. Lawler told the soldier to stop the jeep. Lawler exited the jeep and approached the small store in front of them. He entered the store, seeing only a few customers and the counter clerk, the same clerk that aided Brock earlier.

"I am General Lawler of the United States Military. I am here to ask if any of you have seen this man."

Lawler pulled out a photo of Brock from his coat pocket and held it up for everyone in the shop to see. Most of the customers are confused except for the clerk, for she knows what is going on.

"We just need to know if he came by here. This man is a wanted fugitive. A criminal of the State. He possesses secrets that will destroy all this country is worth if they are revealed. So, tell me now, have any of you seen this man."

The store is quiet, Lawler stood, waiting for someone to answer him. One customer walked over and approached him. Gazing at the photo.

"Have you seen this man?" Lawler said. "If so, say it now."

"No." The customer said. "I've never seen that man in my life. I thought I knew him."

"How so?"

"From a distance, he reminded me of Nathan Hawke."

Lawler shook his head.

"We don't have the time to talk about him. This about Kent Brock's manhunt. I will ask again, have any of you seen him? If so, tell me now and we will be out of your town immediately."

The store is silent, anyone could hear a pen drop inside, with Lawler glaring toward everyone in the store. He nodded, commanding the soldiers to exit the store. Lawler turned back and noticed the clerk somewhat shaking in her steps. He walked over to her, slowly.

"You want something from here, General?" She asked with a trembling voice.

"Why yes. I want to know where Kent Brock has gone?"

"What do you mean? I don't know any Kent Brock. I've never seen the man on that photo you were holding."

"Yes, you have. Tell me now before I have my men come in here and destroy your property. Or I could take you in for aiding a fugitive. That wouldn't look too good now would it."

"No. It wouldn't."

"So, tell me what you know. Now."

After getting himself some sleep, Brock awoke to the sound of someone knocking on the door. James walked over to the door, looking through the peep hole and he opened it, seeing Charlotte standing there. Brock looked over seeing James and Charlotte greet each other. Charlotte walked into the home and seen Brock sitting on the couch.

"Hi, Charlotte."

"Brock, look at you. You look worn out."

"I just have some sleep, so I'll be just fine."

"Now, before you think that I came only to see you, I have some information that may pique your interest to get rid of your 'Beast' problem."

Brock sat up from the couch, interested.

"What do you have? Did the tests finally come in?"

"They did, and I brought the results with me so you can see what they present. It is very interesting."

"Let me see the results, please."

She placed her purse down, pulling out a folder with the results inside. She handed the folder to Brock, who immediately opened the folder and started reading what was inside. He shook his head in disbelief.

"How can this be possible?"

"It has something to do with the radiation that flows through your bloodstream."

"He has radiation in his bloodstream?" James said. "Are

you completely serious?"

"It's not harmful to anyone else, James. Only me."

"It doesn't harm you as you believe. It also created a barrier that protects you from serious diseases and sicknesses."

"But it enabled me to turn into some hairy monster. A monster that I cannot control, even if I wished for the right to do it."

Brock kept reading the results and noticed the word, '*thunderstorm*'. He looked up at Charlotte.

"What thunderstorms have to do with my transformation?"

"Your body is able to sense a storm coming from miles away. The lightning that accompanies a storm will also be attracted to you. A strike from the lightning will cause your body to change into the Beast."

"So, I'm not even safe when it rains."

"At least we're in a snow season right now, man." James said. "I haven't seen any lightning in a snowstorm."

"James, there's thunder snowstorms as well."

James stared for a moment. A smile frozen on his face that slowly faded away.

"Oh. You might as well start staying inside buildings, Kent."

"Physical and mental pain are also factors that will configure your body's transformation process."

"That explains why I changed when I was shot in the leg running through the woods."

"You were shot?!" James said. "Damn, man. You're basically unstoppable."

"Funny."

The military surrounded their base in Montana, where Lawler and his army of soldiers arrived. Getting out of the jeep, he approved the commanding officer at the base. They shook hands and went into the base to talk. Inside, they went and sat down at a table.

"I heard about your little fugitive problem up north."

"I'm aware everyone has heard about it. I'm not liking this guy. He's a fugitive to the government and he has to be brought in."

"Is it true that he can transform into a monster. You know, like a werewolf or something?"

"He doesn't turn into a werewolf. More like a beast. A large, hairy, brute beast. He can barely be stopped. Almost near impossible."

"I heard you lost some of your guys out there as well. The Beast killed them I hear."

"He did."

"I have a guy coming here in a few minutes. I'm going to place him under your wing. Trust me, he can get the job done."

"How so."

They hear a helicopter hovering above the base. They get up from the table and step outside, seeing the chopper above them and inside is the soldier the commanding officer was speaking about.

"A few seconds rather than minutes, General. That's the guy."

Lawler looked at the man in the helicopter as it landed. He

exited the chopper, walking towards the base. An African American man, well fit, his hair shave down almost bald. His eyes filled with a mission to fulfill.

"Who is he?"

"Sean Hancock, one of this country brightest and skilled soldiers in the past decade. He knows his way around the fields of battle and seeks to solve your fugitive problem."

"Is that right?"

Sean approached both Lawler and the officer. They shook hands and greeted each other.

"Hancock. This is General Lawler. The Commando."

"It is an honor to finally meet you, sir."

"I can say the same thing about you after what I've previously heard of you. I hear you want to capture Kent Brock, the fugitive of the State?"

"More than anything, sir. Honestly, I want to capture his other half. The Beast I keep hearing about. Sounds like these soldiers here are afraid of him by the way they speak of him. Well, I'm not and I'm willing to lead a team of yours out to find Brock and smoke him out. End this manhunt period."

Lawler looked at the commanding officer, who is smiling. He turned back to Hancock and extended his hand. They shake hands.

"Fair enough. I will give you some of my men to lead in your mission to find Brock. If you do find him, bring him in. If he transforms, take him down and bring him in."

"I will do what I must, General."

Hancock walked into the base with Lawler and the commanding officer following him. After several hours of searching for any trace of Brock's whereabouts. Lawler walked over to the search team and sat down with them.

"No need on tracking Kent Brock down. I know where he is."

"Where is he, General." Hancock said from a distance.

"He's at a friend's home. James Porter. Find his address and Hancock, lead the team there and take him down."

"Will do, sir."

They receive the address as Hancock prepares his team of soldiers. They exit the base in a pack, gathering in three jeeps with Sean driving one himself. Lawler approached Sean at the jeep.

"Make sure you bring him back, you hear?"

"Loud and clear, General. You'll be seeing Kent Brock or his other half in no time."

Sean drove away with the team following him. Lawler looked on as the jeep went into the street and drove away.

The sun slowly started to set as Kent talks with James and Charlotte in the living room of the home, unaware of Sean's arrival.

"So, what can I do about it? How can I get rid of this thing inside me?"

"You most likely won't be able to."

"What do you mean? I should have an opportunity to find something to rid me of the monster."

"You ever tried siphoning him out?" James said.

"That won't work."

"Just a small suggestion."

"There is a machine down in Dallas. It might have the possibility to reversing the transformation."

"Let's make a trip down there now."

"The machine could also possibly kill you."

"Charlotte, listen to me. I'm being chased down by the government. The world as we know it is changing drastically every day and there are these others out there in different cities that I've heard about that are potentially worse than the monster within me."

Charlotte nodded.

"Let's go down to Dallas and sort all of these problems that I have out. Maybe I can have a normal life it succeeds."

"Or you could die and be gone man." James said. "Won't have to worry about being a fugitive anymore."

"Real funny."

"If that's what you want to do. I'll make the flight arrangements."

"Thank you."

Down in the woods near James' home is Sean and the soldiers in their jeeps. Sean signals out to stop the jeeps and leave them in their present area to make a stealthier attempt toward the home.

"Better the quietness of the forest than the roaring of the jeeps."

They slowly make their move toward the home. Sean noticed the window, three silhouettes standing, talking it seemed to him.

"There's three of them inside. Brock, James, and who's the woman?"

"It might be the General's niece?" A soldier said.

"The General's niece? What is she doing around a

fugitive?"

"He's been warning her not to hang around him for years."

Sean scoffed as he walked closer to the home, particularly the front door.

"Looks like she just found herself some trouble."

"You're not going to shoot her, are you?"

"I'm not here for the General's niece or Brock's little friend. I'm here for the Beast."

"We were commanded to come here and capture Brock. Return him to the base."

"That we will do. But I want to see this Beast first and foremost before turning him in."

They inched closer to the front door of the home with Sean giving out signals for the other soldiers to surround the entire house. Inside the home, Brock feels uncertain as if he knows the home is surrounded.

"We have to go now."

"Why?" James asked.

"They're surrounded the home. They're here."

"Who's here?" Charlotte asked.

"The military."

Sean walked up the set of stairs toward the door, he leaned against the wall, looking at the other soldiers behind him."

"One... Two...Three!"

Sean kicked in the door, frightening Brock, James, and Charlotte. They ducked as the soldiers barged into James' home, running toward Brock, who already jumped out of a window, running into the forest. Sean spotted him and raised up his rifle.

He pointed it toward Brock, aiming for his right calf.

"Don't shoot him! It will cause the transformation!"

Sean looked over at James, smiling.

"That's exactly what I wanted to hear."

"DON'T!" Charlotte said.

Sean took the shot and the bullet flew through Brock's calf. He yelled as he fell to the ground in the snow and dirt. Sean laughed as he jumped out of the window.

"Where are you going, lieutenant?"

"I'm going to see the Beast. Firsthand."

Sean ran through the snowy woods, searching for Brock. Following the blood on the ground.

"I know you're here, Brock. Go ahead and change for me. I want the Beast, not you. You understand that. Give me what I came for."

Sean heard a rustle coming from the trees and spotted Brock leaning against a tree. His eyes slowly glowing a red and gray hair began to stick out of his arms and legs. Brock fell to the ground, painfully transforming into the Beast. Sean laughed with joy, witnessing the transformation right before his eyes.

"Finally." Sean said. "He is here."

The Beast rose up from the ground, with the light of the moon shining on his brute gray hairy body and his long black hair, roaring loudly in the forest, frightening the animals nearby. Sean smiled as he stood before him. The Beast turned and looked down toward Sean, his eyes filled with anger and rage. He growled toward Sean, but Sean doesn't run.

"You don't scare me! I am not these simple men in a uniform! I have faced many odds in my military career. You are just the next step to my glory."

The Beast roared as he grabbed Sean and through him against a tree, potentially breaking the back of Sean in the process. The Beast roared and jumped up into the air, disappearing into the night sky.

III

THE MOUNTAINROCK

The Beast roamed through the woods, knocking down smaller trees and jumping through the air above them. Still enraged and full of anger, the Beast knocked down anything that was in his path. Going through the lands and stopping around the Crazy Mountains.

While running through the woods, a slight clicking sound has made itself known, getting the Beast's attention. The Beast stopped and surveyed his surroundings, seeing nothing but trees and snow.

The Beast growled as the clicking intensified and grew louder. The Beast continued to roar back and from one of the trees, was a figure sitting above him. It was responsible for the clicking sounds. The Beast looked up, seeing and smelling the decayed stench of the figure, which dropped down from the tree onto him, trying to bite him. The Beast threw the figure off and it rammed itself into a tree. The Beast roared at the figure, which stood up and roared back.

The figure stood gaunt and almost skeletal-like. It had an ash-gray complexion body covered with white hair and with sharp teeth and ram-like horns. Its dark red eyes appeared to be pushed deep into its sockets. The figure was a Wendigo. A malevolent creature of Native American Mythology that possesses people and turns them into cannibalistic monsters.

The Wendigo stood facing the Beast. The two monsters ran toward each other. Strength against strength. The Beast slammed the Wendigo into the snow and jumped up in the air, coming to crash onto the Wendigo. The Wendigo moved from the area as the Beast landed on the ground.

The Wendigo screeched as it lunged onto the Beast's back. The Beast tried shaking the Wendigo off as it dug its teeth into the Beast's hide. The Beast roared as he slammed himself to the ground, with the Wendigo beneath him. The Beast turned around and stomped the Wendigo's face into the ground and walked over to a tree. The Beast grabbed the strength and pulled with his strength, the tree out of the ground and slammed it onto the Wendigo. Seemly killing the winter creature. The Beast looked at the Wendigo, not moving, he roared and jumped up into the night sky, disappearing.

Lawler and the military arrive at the scene of James' home. Lawler pulled Charlotte out of the home to speak to her while the soldiers went and searched for Hancock.

"Why did you bother coming here to see him?"

"He need help, Uncle."

"He's a fugitive. He will get all the help he can get behind solid bars and steel doors."

"That won't help him at all. It will only increase his changes of transforming and killing everyone inside the prison."

"You better hope he didn't kill Hancock. If he did, he will have a bigger price to pay rather than being a target."

Lawler walked away from Charlotte, he passed by James and nodded while he walked into the nearby forest along with the soldiers. James walked over to Charlotte.

"Are they going to pay for all the stuff they damaged or what?"

"I don't know. Maybe."

"Maybe, huh. All well, I guess I'll use my paycheck to do it all myself then. Damn military."

Walking in the forest, Lawler gets a signal by the solders to come quickly. He ran through the forest and stopped by the other soldiers, who have found Sean and his back is cracked from the attack of the Beast.

"Take him to the jeep. Carefully now."

The soldiers slowly carry Sean to the jeep as Lawler looked on.

"I have an idea for this problem."

While walking to the jeep, Lawler looked back at Charlotte. With anger, though a caring anger. James walked up to Lawler.

"Are you guys going to pay for my stuff you broke?"

"Back away."

"Sure thing, sir."

Charlotte looked at Lawler with disgust and hatred in her eyes. His hatred for Brock has caused a problem for the both.

"Go home. Leave this place and go back to work. We will find him and bring him in."

"You're not listening, Uncle."

"No! You're not listening! You're blinded to this man. You know what he can become. You've seen the Beast for yourself. What it can do to a human being. What it could do to you if you keep staying so damn close to him."

"I will be fine. He will not harm me."

"Keep hanging around him and see what happens. Maybe you'll figure it out that way."

Lawler and the military leave James' property, going into the forest on the road. James shook his head.

"Damn military man."

"He won't listen. We have to find Kent ourselves before they do."

"Where would Kent go?"

"Dallas. I believe he's going to Dallas."

"You mean the Beast is going to Dallas. Are you even sure that's where he's going?"

"I know that's where he's going."

Charlotte entered her car and looked out at James.

"Make sure you're ready for flying."

"Like I have any other choice."

Still roaming through the wilderness and the sky, The Beast stopped and jump up again past a sign saying, 'Welcome to Colorado". He let out a loud roar before continuing into Colorado.

Lawler and the military have placed Sean inside one of their hospitals to be checked on. The doctors state that Sean may never be able to walk again due to the amount if nerve damage to his back. Lawler looked at Sean, seeing him awake. He entered the room.

"General." Sean said. "Pleasure to see you."

"Same here. So, they told you about your back?"

"They did. But that's not going to stop me."

"You can't walk anymore according to what they've told you. What can you do for us anymore. You're out."

"No. No I'm not."

"How so?"

"You already know. The formula. The same formula that transformed Brock into the Beast. Inject me with it and you'll see what I can really do."

"I'm afraid I can't do that to you."

"Why not?!"

"Because you're not fit for the army anymore, son."

"Give me the formula, General and you will see your fugitive taken down. Him and his Beast."

Lawler sighed. He thought to himself for the moment. His eyes gazing toward Sean. Concerned for his health and living.

"Are you sure about this?"

"I am."

"If this goes wrong, it could kill you."

Sean laughed.

"What else do I have left in this world anyway. If I die, so be it. If I survive, welcome to your revived soldier."

Lawler nodded and signaled the doctors. He told the

doctors of the formula and they go through security to receive it from the secured locker. The doctors walk into the room with the formula and the radiation machine, the same machine Charlotte told Brock about.

"This machine will allow the formula to transfer into your bloodstream, giving you the possibly of possessing the same feats as Kent Brock's other half."

"Beautiful. The power of the Beast in the palm of my hand."

The doctors placed the machine around Sean on the table. They prepared the needles and injection tubes tied into his arms. They turn the machine on, it roared as Lawler stared at Sean.

"Are you ready?" Lawler asked.

"I am, General. Get on with it."

Lawler nodded, signaling the doctors to start the procedure.

The process started with first injecting a small dose of radiation into Sean's body and afterwards the formula flowed through the tubes, entering his bloodstream. Sean grunted as the procedure was very, very painful. Waiting for the remainder of the formula to enter his bloodstream, Lawler worried if Sean would die on the table as he was going in and out of consciousness.

"He can make it through this." Lawler said to himself. "I know he can."

"He's going out." The doctor said. "We have to take it off of him now."

"No." Lawler said. "Let it finish first. Then, you can take remove it."

"He might be dying, sir."

"He knew the risks before he accepted the procedure. He's a strong man. He'll overcome this. I promise you on that."

The procedure started to slow down. The doctors waited within the seconds for Sean to wake up. Lawler stood still, waiting patiently for Sean to respond to him and the doctors. Within seconds, Sean jumped up, back to conscious. He looked around the room.

"Is it finished?"

"It is. How do you feel?"

"I feel incredible. Almost as if I have strength that I've never possessed before. It's strange."

Sean moved the equipment and stepped from the table. Standing on his own two feet. His back completely healed. The doctors are astonished at the sight of what they are witnessing.

"This is incredible." The doctor said. "Never seen anything like it."

"You will keep this indoors if you want to keep your life free from threats."

"Yes sir."

Lawler looked at Sean, seeing the intensity in his eyes. His body slowly beginning to morph.

"Sean, you're transforming."

"I know!"

Sean fell to the ground, yelling in pain, but with little laughter mixed in with his screams as his body slowly started to transform. Instead of gray hair coming from his body, a dark brownish hide started to form from his body, looking like rocks and minerals carved from the mountains. Lawler stood back from the room as the doctor gazed on, seeing Sean transform into a monster unlike the Beast. Sean grew in height, taller than the Beast and physically stronger. Sean's transformation was complete, and he appeared to be made of solid rock.

"He looks like a rock monster." The doctor said.

"No." Lawler said. "He's something else."

"Ah!" Sean said in a deep pitched graveling voice. "This is beautiful. The power surges through me. I've never felt something like this before. Look at me, I can move mountains with my strength. I am truly the rock which will decimate the Beast."

"Are you all right, Sean?" Lawler said.

"Sean? Sean is gone, General. You may call me the Mountainrock."

"The Mountainrock it is." Lawler said, nodding. "Are you ready for the mission?"

"I am. I can sense where he's heading. He's going down south. Ah. I know where's he's going."

Mountainrock walked out of the room and toward the exit doors. Lawler followed him.

"General, gather your men. We're going to Texas."

Mountainrock opened the doors and jumped into the air, moving at quick speed. Lawler rallied up his soldiers as they entered helicopters and flew up in the air, heading for Texas. Also, in a plane heading to Texas is James and Charlotte. They are prepared for what they are about to witness.

IV

<u>BATTLE OF DALLAS</u>

During the day after the official rally began, Mountainrock made his landfall in Vernon, Texas. Using his newly heightened senses to track down The Beast's last movements. He found his footsteps in a field near the country lands.

"He was here. He was here. He's going further south."

Moutainrock jumped into the air, leaving Vernon as Lawler and his team attempted to keep up with him.

"Who's the giant rock man, General?" A soldier asked hesitantly.

"That rock man was formerly known as Sean Hancock. Now, he goes by name of The Mountainrock."

James and Charlotte arrive in Dallas. They leave the airport, going straight for the laboratory that the radiation machine is located.

"We have to get there before my Uncle shows up."

"You think they're coming down here?"

"Again. I know they are."

In the outskirts of Fort Worth, The Beast arrived, roaring loudly as he jumped into the air, going straight for Dallas. James and Charlotte arrive at the laboratory and find out the machine was taken. Taken by the military, which was used to turn Sean into Mountainrock.

"Damn it! They got here before we did."

"Maybe there's another way we can help Kent. I'm sure there are more than one of those machines."

"There were only three developed. One was here. The other two are in China and Russia."

"Over there, huh. Well, I didn't know they were creating their own Beasts too. Are they making a Beast army or something?"

"I don't know. We have to prepare for Kent's arrival anyway. Whether he's Kent or whether he's The Beast."

"Ok."

Mountainrock, Lawler, and his team arrive in Dallas. They look around the location with Mountainrock uses his senses even more.

"Mountainrock snarled. "Determination."

"What have you found so far?" Lawler said.

"He's here, General. He's here in the city. He went left."

Lawler looked to the left with his binoculars, recognizing the buildings and the streets.

"He's going to his lab."

"Great." Mountainrock said. "Give him a welcome home party."

"Where are you going?"

"I'm going downtown. I want him to see me in my new glory."

Mountainrock jumped away and out if sight as Lawler and the army moved down the streets of Dallas. They moved and went straight for the laboratory.

Inside the lab, Charlotte and James sat, waiting on Brock to arrive. Hour after minutes after seconds. They sat, waiting patiently and calm.

"Are you sure he's going to be here?" James asked.

"I'm positive."

They heard engines roaring from the outside. They knew without hesitation it isn't Kent. Charlotte ran toward the doors to lock them, but they are kicked in by the soldiers lead by Lawler. She looked at him with rage. James stood still with his hands up in the air.

"Nice to see you all again." James said. "Have you come to donate to the cause preferably named, *The James Porter Cause*? Where you guys destroyed my shit."

A soldier went up and clocked James in the head with the butt of his machine gun. Charlotte witnessed it and looked at Lawler.

"This isn't necessary."

"It is necessary. Where's Brock?"

"We don't know. He hasn't shown up."

Lawler nodded.

"Well, when he does, we will take him out and you will watch in horror as to what becomes of him."

"No."

"Take her and her friend away from this place."

The soldiers grabbed Charlotte and James, pulling them from the laboratory. Charlotte screamed at Lawler. He looked at her.

"Shut her up for me please!"

The soldier slapped Charlotte as she tried to fight back with the soldier. While the chaos inside the lab, a distant roar is heard, stopping the rage inside the lab. James looked up at the ceiling, smiling.

"He's here. You guys are screwed."

The ceiling collapses on the soldiers and standing there is The Beast, who roars toward Lawler. He yelled to his soldiers to attack him with their weapons.

"Take him down!"

The Beast roared as he destroyed nearly every soldier in the lab. Lawler stepped back from the chaos, trying to leave the lab. Charlotte followed him with James behind her, trying to watch The Beast defeat the soldiers.

"Kick their asses, Kent!"

The Beast turned to James and roared at him, in turn causing James to run out of the lab, following Charlotte. Outside of the lab, The Beast rammed through the walls and destroyed the jeeps and their loaded weapons. Leaving Lawler and his team defenseless, The Beast approached Lawler and stared at him.

"He's waiting for you downtown." Lawler said.

The Beast roared at him before leaping into the air, towards downtown. Charlotte and James watch as The Beast leaped toward downtown.

"We have to follow him." Charlotte said.

"Let's go."

They get into one of the remaining jeeps and drive away from the lab. Lawler stood up, running after them.

"Get back here!"

Downtown Dallas is covered with civilians as Mountainrock stood in the streets, destroying cars and property. He did it out of joy and impatience.

"Where is The Beast? Where is he?!"

The Dallas police arrive and attempt to take down Mountainrock by shooting him. Only their bullets deflected off of Mountainrock's rough, rocky hide. He smiled at them.

"Amusing you are. Petty weapons."

Mountainrock grabbed the police car and slammed it into the others as he swiped the officers and threw them into buildings and windows. A crash is sounded from the distance away from Mountainrock. He looked over to the site and seen The Beast standing, facing him with his red eyes piercing into his. Mountainrock smiled.

"Ah. The Unstoppable Beast."

The Beast took a few steps before roaring loudly at

Mountainrock with rage following. Mountainrock laughed as he started walking toward The Beast.

"Finally. A challenge that I have been waiting for."

Mountainrock started to pace and so did The Beast. The two monsters ran toward each other, prepared to battle one another. The Beast lunged in the air and so did Mountainrock, with civilians running around them in fear. Mountainrock speared The Beast and threw him into a nearby eighteen-wheeler truck, causing it to explode. The Beast flipped out of the exploding truck and laid on the road. Mountainrock walked over to him, grinning.

"Show me your true power!"

The Beast looked around and grabbed pieces of a car. Mountainrock ran toward him, roaring. The Beast ran to him with the car pieces and started smashing him with it. The Beast gave Mountainrock an uppercut, knocking him down as The Beast pummeled him into the road, creating a miniature crater with his strength.

The Beast grabbed Mountainrock by his throat and pounded his fist into Mountainrock's face. Mountainrock laughed the punch off.

"You're holding back. You're afraid of me!"

Mountainrock kicked The Beast off of him and into the air, where he lunged up toward him and tackled him down to the ground, near the outskirts of Dallas. Not many civilians are seen in the outskirts as Mountainrock walked over toward The Beast and grabbed him, holding him up by his throat.

"I am stronger than you! I am better than you! I am The Mountain made of invincible rock."

Mountainrock tossed The Beast against a nearby

construction building and held him against the wall, choking him.

"You don't deserve such a power to possess. I deserve it and much more!"

The Beast kneed Mountainrock and punched him in the gut and face, but it didn't faze him. Mountainrock slammed The Beast to the ground and kneed him in the face. Mountainrock laughed as he walked away, seeing Charlotte and James arrive at the scene.

"How did they get over here? Never mind."

Mountainrock walked over to Charlotte and James. They feared for their lives, backing up against the jeep.

"What the hell is that thing?" James asked. "A rock Beast?"

"It's Hancock." Charlotte said. "Look at the way he moves. His behavior shines right off of him."

"You know your people, Ms. Lawler. Allow men to finish your friend off and afterwards, I will deal with you and your alley here."

Charlotte pulled out a gun, to which Mountainrock swiped it from her hand. Laughing at her.

"Any last words for Kent Brock."

The Beast stood up and roared at Mountainrock, with his arms wide apart.

"No one defeats The Beast!!!"

The Beast slammed his hands together to create a shockwave in the air, knocking Mountainrock into the building. Charlotte and James took cover by the jeep. The Beast ran over to Mountainrock and grabbed him by the neck, holding tightly. He choked out Mountainrock and stomped him in his chest, defeating him in the process. The Beast roared as he slowly transformed back into Brock.

"Kent!" James said. "You're back!"

"Let's help him up." Charlotte said. "Get him away from this place."

They helped him up and placed him inside the jeep, driving away, seeing as they could avoid further confrontations with the military.

Lawler searched Dallas for The Beast and was unsuccessful in finding him. He later received a call stating that some agency came across Mountainrock and have taken him to a secure prison facility. Lawler demanded to know the agency's name and the name of the agency was T.I.T.A.N.

"Those guys again." Lawler said to himself, hanging up the phone.

After several days had passed, the government paid for all of James' damages and Charlotte went back to her workings in her laboratory.

In the outskirts of a small town, Kent is walking down the street and is approached by an unknown man, wearing a black suit with a dark blue tie and sunglasses. The unknown man told Kent he knew how he was and how he could transform into The Beast. The man only told Kent that something is about to happen, and the world could be at its end, leaving Kent to wonder what the man was talking about and what is coming to the earth.

I

WE NEED A TEAM

A helicopter landed on the front side of the base. From out of the helicopter walked out Colonel Evan Nader. Inside the T.I.T.A.N. Headquarters base, Nader walked through the hallway, removing his black sunglasses and opened the stairs door. He takes he steps down, going near the basement area of the headquarters. Nader opened the bottom door and enters what appeared to be a secret laboratory facility that only a few within T.I.T.A.N. know about. Nader walked through the lab, seeing over a dozen scientists and agents inside working on various projects ranging from nuclear weapons to uncovering mythological artifacts and studying them.

One table had the artifact made of ore with its shiny golden color, the same artifact that J had in his possession before he was defeated by The Swordman. Nader walked over to one table and on the table was an artifact of ancients past. Standing by the table were two agents and Jessica Mara, one of T.I.T.A.N.'s most highly trained agents, standing by the table wearing her dark blue and black uniform with her brown hair down to her shoulders. She approached Nader with confidence as to what they have discovered.

"Agent Mara. Unusual to see you down here."

"I was reported to come here to see this artifact that the agents from outside have discovered."

"What artifact is it?"

"According to its ancient language. Presumably ancient Hebrew language. This is the legendary Holy Artifact of Life."

"The Holy Artifact of Life?" Nader asked. "What kind of life?"

"From what we're read of its history, there's someone currently residing inside of it. Someone who the ancients were terrified of."

"You mean to tell me inside this tablet of stone is a living person?"

"Not a person. A god."

"A Dark God from what the scrolls have said." Jessica said. "The scrolls state that this Dark God ruled the earth for a millennium before being overthrown and placed inside this stone. It is prophesized that the stone will one day break, freeing him from his current prison."

Nader looked down at the artifact and gaze toward the agents. He stared at them deeply with some concern.

"You two take special care of this thing. You understand?"

"Yes sir."

Jessica walked over to Nader, asking to speak in quiet. Nader agreed and the two walked toward the stairs, away from the scientists and agents.

"We need to take the artifact back to its previous location."

"What gives you that idea, Agent Mara?"

"Because if an accident occurs, this Dark God who is trapped inside will come out and will more likely kill us all. The scientists aren't prepared for something like that. Neither is the world."

"The artifact is safer here than it would be out there in the open. What would happen if our enemies, ADDER, V.A.U.L.T., or Glasco had their hands on it. Imagine what they could do with it."

Nader looked up and seen Professor John Flm walking inside the lab. Nader decided to approach him, concerning with the matters of the artifact. Flm turned around, seeing Nader and Mara walking toward him.

"I see you're here."

"Professor, what do you know of that artifact on the table there?"

"I do know that it possesses great power within it as well as outside of it."

"What do you mean, outside?" Nader said.

"Well, think of it as a gateway into the other dimensions. Someone or something on the other side could sense the artifact's aura and could potentially open up a portal, leaving their world and entering ours."

The Artifact shakes on the table suddenly. Moving on its own, rumbling and trembling, almost shattering the table itself. The scientists and other agents leave the lab, except for Nader, Mara, and Flm accompanied by a few of their trained agents. They stared at the artifact, seeing it beginning to glow. The golden ore artifact also starts to glow and the two shine brightly, almost blinding Nader and company. From the front of the artifacts appeared a portal, inside the portal was nothing but darkness, you could see the stars of space when gazing deeper into it.

"The hell is going on?" Nader said.

The portal exploded as Nader and company covered themselves from the small blast. The room is silent as they look up toward the artifact, seeing two individuals sitting before them.

One was a man, holding a spear, was covered in dark green and gold apparel. His long black hair shined darkly before them. He isn't human. The other individual was a woman, wearing all black with her black hair, accompanied by her violet highlights. They both raised their glances toward Nader and company. The two, both figures of destruction and chaos across the earth and the universe. Noldar and Death.

"Mr., what we need you to do right now is put down the spear. Ma'am, stay where you are, and we'll speak to you in a minute."

"A minute?!" Death asked with a smile. "We won't need a minute."

Death laughed at Nader. She turned to Noldar, who smiled back. Noldar jumped into the air and attacked the agents inside the lab, impaling them with his spear and firing out energy beams from the spear. Death approached some agents and stabbed them in their chest with her knife and a couple of death crosses. Nader, Mara, and Flm stood close to each other as Noldar and Death killed the agents inside the lab, turning their eyes toward them.

"This doesn't have to get any worse." Nader mentioned.

"Sure it does. Do you know who I am. I am Noldar of Eragard. I come here to your world with a major purpose and reason."

"You're the nemesis of Theus." Flm said. "You're real!"

"I am. Kneel to me in my glory and give me the praise that I deserve."

"I'm afraid he will not."

Nader looked toward Death. He recognized her from the photos and information he's received over the past few months. He pointed at her and nodded, while she smiled at him.

"I know who you are." Nader said. "Your presence doesn't confuse me."

"I'm sure. Everyone knows who I am."

"I'm wondering how soon he'll find out you've escaped Pegasus."

"He will have time to worry about me later. Right now, it's just you and us."

Noldar approached the table and grabbed the artifacts,

warping them into miniature objects, able to put inside a pocket. Nader looked at what he seen and was astonished at Noldar's power. Death looked toward Noldar and the tables.

"Do you have them?"

"I do. Shall we leave this place of filth?"

"We shall do so."

Death pulled out a gun from her coat and shot Nader in the chest. He fell to the ground as Death and Noldar left the room with Mara following them. Flm stayed with Nader, calling for assistant. Mara ran up the stairs and into the hallway, she ran outside of the base, seeing Death and Noldar inside one of their helicopters, flying away from the base. Downstairs, Nader gets to his feet, revealing he was wearing a bulletproof vest underneath his shirt.

"I'm fine, Professor. I'll be just fine."

Nader looked around, not seeing Mara.

"Where did Agent Mara go?"

"She went upstairs after them."

Nader ran upstairs and went outside, seeing Mara looking up into the clouds. She turned around, seeing Nader walking and the bulletproof vest he was wearing. Relieved, she pointed up into the air.

"They've escaped sir."

"Damn. And they have the artifacts. Both of them."

Flm walked out of the base, standing behind Nader and Mara.

"What are we going to do, Colonel?"

Nader turned to him and walked back into the base, standing around the remaining agents inside.

"Everyone, listen to me. This is a Code 6. War has come."

Nader looked at Mara.

"Contact them. Tell them it's time."

"Yes sir."

Somewhere at an undisclosed location, appeared to be an abandoned building, formerly belonging to a company called Fargo Railways. Death and Noldar sit inside of it at a table. The two artifacts are laying on top of the table. The doors of the building open and Kex Kendrick entered with Beatrice behind him. Wearing his known white suit with his blonde hair combed down.

"Ah!" Death clapped. "You made it! The son of a bitch made it!"

"So, it's you." Kendrick said. "You're the woman who contacted me?"

"I am."

Kendrick looked over at Noldar. Confused about his wardrobe. His apparel disturbs him.

"Who the hell is this guy?"

"Show respect, worm. I am Noldar of Eragard. The rightful King of Eragard. Once I claim my throne that is."

Death shook her head at Noldar. Amused by his words.

"Your ambition is little, Noldar. Like a child begging for bread."

"Ok. So, you're part of this agreement too. We all have common enemies?"

"Yes, we do, Kex." Death said. "Now is the time to kill them all."

Kendrick grabbed a chair and sat down at the table, staring at the artifacts. He pointed toward them with enthusiasm in his eyes.

"Are those what I think they are?"

"They are Kex." Death said. "My brother is inside the largest one and we're going to break him out."

"And he will be the one to finally solve all our problems?"

"Oh, yes. My brother is very, very, very powerful. An ancient of the ancients."

"He can do more than solve our problems." Noldar

mentioned. "He can give us the desires of our hearts."

"Is that right?" Kex asked. "I like this guy already."

They all sat at the table, gazing at the artifacts. Kex smiled with curiosity. Noldar smirked with conquest and Death clapped her hands, excited.

"So, when do we begin?" Noldar grinned.

"Let's get this party started right now!" Death yelled. "Come on! Let's go out there and cause hell upon them that come against us!"

"Patience is a virtue, Death." Kex said. "We need a proper plan in order for all of our goals to meet without any interruptions."

"I understand what you're saying, Kex. I do. But I want to do this now!"

"We all want to do this now. I will see what I can do in some of your major cities. As long as the Thunder God doesn't appear, our plans will succeed."

"I surely hope they do. We'll have to get rid of this titagod firsthand. He could seriously destroy our plans if he finds out about them before we set them in motion."

Death looked at them both, shaking her head as if she's waiting for them to speak of someone else. Something that she is familiar with.

"Nice to hear your concerns, but, aren't you guys forgetting about someone."

"Who?" Kex and Noldar both asked.

"The Swordman."

"I hear he's nothing more than some folklore told to frighten children." Kex said. "Like the Bogeyman."

"The Bogeyman is not a folktale, Kendrick of Earth."

"Neither is The Swordman. We have to be prepared."

"I am prepared. How about the two of you?"

"I am." Noldar said.

"I'm always prepared." Death said. "What else should we talk about? Dinner?"

Beatrice reached over to Kex at the table. She gets close to him, as if she's concerned about his current place inside the building around Death and Noldar.

"Are you sure you can trust these people, Kex?"

"They will be no problem, Beatrice. Anything goes wrong and you have it covered."

"Sure thing, sir."

II

SEARCHING FOR THE RECRUITS

Nader goes out to speak with Kenari Clark and Nathan Hawke in Retropolis and Newark, New Jersey individually. He tells them about the incident that has taken place at the headquarters and asked them if they're involved in aiding him, since the artifacts could be used to destroy the planet itself. Kenari later went to visit Hawke, the two talked about Nader's meetings and the two have to go out and speak with others that Nader had in mind to talk with. After defeating the Black Sector in Toronto, Commander Norland had met with Hawke, discussing the *Resistance Protocol*, with Norland prepared to join in for the safety of the planet.

Kenari traveled to Detroit, Michigan to speak with a candidate that Nader seemed to be able to persuade into joining the team. He approached the home of the candidate, knocking on the door. The door opened and standing there is the candidate. Kenari realized who the man was and has heard of the history.

"Mr. Dameon Mason. I take it you know who I am."

"I know who you are. Why are you here visiting me?"

"Colonel Evan Nader of T.I.T.A.N. has chosen you to be a possible candidate for his team to combat a major threat to the planet."

Mason shook his head and nodded. Kenari stared at him, studying his body language. Sensing that he doesn't like what he is hearing. Mason giggled quietly to himself.

"I can sense you find this very amusing."

"You can say that. Because I already are aware that the Nano Man is involved in this somehow. The showoff he is."

"I wouldn't say that to be exact, but he is involved with this."

Mason stepped out from the door, revealing his bionic arms and lower legs. Kenari stared at him and fully knew who he was.

"You're the man that survived the terrible explosion during the war."

"I am and as I'm sure you already know, Nathan Hawke was responsible for me losing my limbs. I don't take it lightly and he aids the Nano Man. Sorry, but tell Nader that I decline his offer and will help on my own terms. I will not be siding on a team with Hawke or his Nano Man puppet."

"I respect your decision, Mason." Kenari said. "It's been a pleasure."

Kenari turned and walked away from the home. Mason watched him as he left the site. Mason closed his door.

Later on during the day, Kenari traveled to Chicago, Illinois to visit John Terror. Kenari found him completing one of his missions, investigating the mysterious disappearance of several people involved in an organization called Agency X. Terror turned around, seeing Kenari approach him.

"It's been a while and yet I see you again."

"It was only a matter of time."

The two shake hands and they stand and talk to one another, surrounded by dead bodies that Terror has recently killed.

"I see you have been at work out here."

"I have. Something is going on and its very strange. An agency came to this city and is taking people. The police won't do anything about it, so as always, I am lending my hand into this investigation."

One man stood up slowly, trying to run away. Terror turned and spotted him. He pulled out his gun and shot the man in the back, killing him. Kenari nodded with a smirk.

"A good shot."

"Needed when its necessary. So, why are you here? Must be important."

"It is. A major threat is coming to the planet and it could very well be the end of us all."

"You know this was already set in motion, don't you?"

"I am aware of the times we're living in. They reveal all that we were prepared to do."

"So, is this some kind of team you're talking about? I mean, if it is, then who's already on board?"

"So far, myself and the Nano Man."

"You two teaming up, huh. Interesting dynamic there. Funny as well, because you're not even supposed to be around people like him. Those are the people who make this world sick and hungry."

"I understand where I need to be and the people I fellowship with. What do you say of the team? Are you in or are you out?"

"Here. If you see me during the big battle, I'm in. If you don't see me, I'm out."

Kenari nodded with a smile.

"Always keeping it a mystery, I see."

"You're the one to talk. The world believes you're a myth. A folklore told to children to make them listen to their parents or ear their vegetables."

"I'm a folklore told to frighten them. Not make them obey their parents. Their parents even fear me."

Terror looked around and walked away from Kenari, pointing

at him with a smirk.

"Remember, if you see me or if you don't. The decision will be made."

"I will wait and see if you keep your word."

Terror gets onto his motorcycle and rides off onto the road. Kenari shook his head, walking away from the location.

Before the day is done, Kenari gets into his jet and flies over to Las Vegas, Nevada. Where he goes to a casino ran by an Asher Dale, CEO of Quantum Industries. Inside the casino, he searched for Asher and later found him outside of the place, near his car. He approached him slowly. Seeing him wearing a suit with his brown cut hair and goatee.

"Asher Dale." Kenari said.

He turned around, seeing Kenari. He smiled at him and hugged him.

"Kenari Clark! It is a pleasure to see you hear."

"Likewise. I need to have a word with you in private. If you don't mind."

"Sure. Let's go to my office and talk."

The two enter the casino and go up to Asher's office. Inside his office is covered with newspaper articles of a 'Archer hero' running around Las Vegas. Kenari noticed the newspaper clippings and articles. He smiled.

"You seem to be in love with yourself."

"What can I say. I sit here while people out there spend all of their money trying to beat my machines while I go out into the city by night, saving their possessions from the rich and the greedy."

"A Robin Hood of Las Vegas is what you are."

"We're both considered myths, my friend. They call me Robin Hood, while they call you the Bogeyman."

"It isn't funny."

"I know it isn't. But, sometimes you have to laugh at their statements. They have no ideas what we do for them on a daily basis."

Asher takes a sip of whisky from his desk and looked at Kenari.

"What is it that we have to discuss with one another, friend?"

"There is a threat coming to earth and a team needs to be united. Nader gave me a list of potential candidates that he had in mind and you're one of them."

"What number am I on the list?"

"What does that matter?"

"Because, whatever number I am shows how much Nader needs me. So, what's the number, Ken?"

"You're number three."

"Horseshit."

"Number three, Oliver. I'm not lying to you."

"That's not fair, you know."

"At least you're on his list."

Oliver nodded with pride.

"Eh, you're right. So, Nader needs my decision on if I'm joining his team or not? That's why you're here?"

"That is the reason why I'm talking to you inside a casino in Las Vegas."

"Tell you what. Tell Nader that I'm on board for the team and I will show up when the time is right for me to show up."

"You always like surprising people."

"It's a specialty of mine."

The two shake hands as Kenari leaves Oliver's casino. Oliver, inside his office turned around and stared at one newspaper article on the wall, showing a photo of himself with the title, "*The Q-Arrow Strikes Again*" on the top. He smiled.

"I'll be there, alright. Bank on it."

Kenari returned to the T.I.T.A.N. Headquarters, seeing Hawke present, walking down the hallway with Commander Norland behind him. They see Kenari and walk toward him, greeting him.

"Look who has shown their face!" Hawke said. "He's here people! He's here!"

"I take it you did your task well?" Kenari said.

"Apparently, this guy knows how to listen to people."

Norland extended his hand out to Kenari. They shake hands, meeting each other for the very first time.

"Nice to meet you, Mr. Clark." Norland said.

"Same here, Commander. I take it you have joined Nader's little team of heroes?"

"I'm only in to protect the people of this planet. Other than that, I probably wouldn't have joined in."

"I see your point there."

Norland looked at Kenari, he thought to himself why would Kenari be part of them team. He looked at Hawke and turned back to Kenari.

"If I may ask you, Mr. Clark, with all respect. Why are you part of Nader's team?"

Hawke turned to Norland, laughing at what he said. Hawke tapped Norland on his shoulders while laughing hysterically. Kenari only stared at Hawke.

"You mean you don't know who Kenari is?" Hawke gestured. "My God!"

"It just appeared strange to see someone like you take part in something like this."

"It happens at certain events. It's not a surprise to me."

Norland looked at Hawke. He turned back to Kenari, still trying to figure how who he is and why he is on the team.

"So, who are you?" Norland asked. "Truly?"

"Commander, listen and listen closely. Kenari Clark is The

Swordman."

Norland looked at Kenari. Staring at him. Hawke stayed quiet, taking in the moment.

"You're the Swordman of Retropolis?"

"I am."

"I thought he was only a myth."

"Just like everyone else who lives on this earth." Hawke said. "Now you're on the other side of things, Commander. You know more than the people know. The Swordman is real and he's standing right in front of you."

"I heard about the incident that took place with the three monsters. A Bird-Thing, a Bigfoot, and an Immortal Werewolf?"

"That's what they were. Me and my allies defeated them and saved the city from further destruction."

"Congratulations on that."

"Same to you from saving Toronto against the Indian. I hear he's been sent to a secure facility."

"Someplace they call Hellgate Haven."

"That doesn't sound like a good place to visit or to live." Hawke said. "Where do they get these names from."

Kenari pulled out Nader's list from his pocket and Hawke noticed it and was already in motion to ask if anyone else accepted Nader's recruitment. Norland looked over, seeing Nader inside an office with General Sarge Hunter.

"So, who on that list accepted to be on the team?"

"Realistically, none of them."

"Seriously."

"Mason declined because you were involved. Terror stated that he will show up or not during the fight. Asher said he agreed to join, but wouldn't tell me when he will show up either."

"They know about the threat that's on its way here, right?"

"Yeah. They are aware of the threat."

"They'll come when they want to come." Norland said. "They

don't know how serious all of this is to the earth."

"They know." Hawke said. "They probably just don't give a damn."

Kenari also noticed Nader inside the office with Hunter. He balled up the list and tossed it into a trash can against the wall.

"Once Nader finishes up with Hunter, we'll have to speak with him. There's no telling where Death and her allies are and what they are up to."

"I can't wait to see Death." Hawke said. "How is she in person? What would you rate her?"

"I'm not talking about this, Nate."

"Come on, Kenari. You're telling me you never thought about it?"

"Never. She is the kind of woman that will take a man, skin him alive and place the skin back on him while he's breathing his final breath."

Up in northern Montana, Kent Brock is residing with his friend, James Porter at his home while preparations are being made for Brock to have a place of his own. Brock's clothes are sitting near him in a small closet. Along with some of his other belongings that he brought back with him from Dallas, Texas. Brock later hears about Nader's plan of recruiting a team to face a threat that's coming to earth.

Believing that he is the threat Nader is talking about, Brock decides to stay secluded inside James' home. James walked into the room, seeing Brock on the computer, tracking T.I.T.A.N.'s movements across the country.

"Why are you watching that, man?"

"I'm just trying to keep track on where they're going."

"I don't think they're coming back here after what they had to go through."

"You're sure about that, James? Are you positive of that?"

"Not really. But it is a possibility."

"You're not talking about me, are you?"

"No. I'm talking about the time those military bastards came in here and destroyed most of my shit. They know better now not to come here."

Kent smiled as James sat next to him, drinking a beer.

"I know that I have been on their watch list ever since the first transformation. This team that he's building, they could very well take me out if they get the opportunity."

"Kent, look. They're not coming for you, all right. Just calm yourself down a bit. Charlotte would've called and told you that they were coming for you, if they were."

"How is she?"

"She's doing good. Still working on finding a new laboratory after you and the military destroyed the other one."

"It wasn't me."

"Fine. The Beast and the military. It's still your body, you know."

"Aware of that every day when I look in the mirror. Funny thing is, when I look in the mirror, I know deep down that he's looking back at me and is clawing his way to come out and kill me.

"You're sure about that?"

"I'm positive. Sometimes, the Beast just wants to get out. Some days, I have to force him to stay inside and calm. Trust me, James, it's not something I would wish on any man."

Nader and Hunter are still talking with each other inside the office. They're discussing the idea of Nader's team and Hunter is disagreeing with it, stating that Nader could've had Norland lead his team against Death and Noldar. Nader tells him that

Norland's team is not prepared for a threat such as Death and Noldar.

"You know with the right training, they could take those fools down."

"I know that and there is no time for training. Death and Noldar are out there plotting a way to take us down and end this world. Training is not an option at this point, General."

"This team of yours, it's a one-time deal or something?"

"This team, if they're successful, which I believe they can and will be, will open the door for more possibilities than I ever imagined."

Hunter sighed as he sat back in the chair. He exhaled and looked at Nader before taking a peek through the window, seeing Kenari, Hawke, and Norland talking with each other.

"I think they want a word with you."

Nader looked out of the window, seeing Hawke signaling him to come to them to talk. Nader nodded and looked back at Hunter, who only stared and stayed quiet.

"Apparently so."

Nader left the office and approached them in the lobby area, where they were standing. Nader looked at Norland and gazed over at Hawke.

"Did you accept the offer, Commander."

"Yes sir. I am onboard with the mission."

Nader nodded and turned to Kenari.

"It's strange to see you in this building. Not your style I take it."

"I'm more of a secluded type of man."

"How did you task go in talking with the candidates?"

"Mason declined because of Hawke's involvement and his anger toward the government and their political games. Terror said he will show up during the battle. Asher agreed, but didn't tell me when he was coming to speak with us concerning the missions.”

“I understand and respect their decisions. Right now, what I need for the three of you to do is get yourselves ready. It seems that you’ll on a mission tonight.”

“What mission, sir?” Norland said.

“We have a small lead on the artifacts.”

“Who has the artifacts in their possession?” Norland said. “Someone from ADDER?”

“No. Individuals worse than ADDER.”

Nader walked into his office with Kenari, Hawke, and Norland following him. He opened up a board, revealing Death and Noldar. Kenari stood still as Hawke and Norland was intrigued.

“She’s in on this.” Kenari said.

“Yeah. I figured how you would react finding out she escaped from Pegasus.”

“I’m sending her back. I can’t sit here while she’s out there freely doing what she pleases.”

“That’s why I have a mission for you and Hawke. Tonight, I need the two of you to find Death and Noldar, bring them in for interrogation.”

Hawke nodded.

“I like it.”

“I don’t. I prefer to handle Death alone.”

“Do with this mission as you please, Mr. Clark. You guys can return to your residences and prepare yourself for the mission at hand. Commander Norland, I have one mission for you, and it concerns a one Kex Kendrick.”

“Kex Kendrick. The arrogant prick from Enigma City? The owner of Kendrick Corporations?”

“I thought it was called KexInc.?” Hawke said. “That’s what the billboards suggest.”

“Well, here in Canada, the name is Kendrick Corporations,

Mr. Hawke." Nader said. "It's still the same damn corporation.

Hawke shrugged his shoulders.

"Besides that, we have found some recent evidence of Mr. Kendrick being a helping hand with Death and Noldar. They've made some sort of agreement it seems."

Kenari walked toward the door, preparing to leave the base.

"I will contact you when I return to Retropolis and I will find Death."

"Sure thing, Kenari." Hawke said. "I'll be leaving as well. Have to tell Alice about this whole thing. She won't like it, but it'll have to do."

Hawke leaves the base, leaving only Nader and Norland standing in the lobby together. Nader smiled.

"You see what I have to go through."

"I thought it was somewhat pleasing for you to hang around guys like that. Especially Hawke. The guy's a talker."

"Can't shut up for the life of him."

Norland laughed.

In Newark, New Jersey, Hawke arrived into the city, going straight to his manor. He arrived at his manor, greeting Derek Willis, his personal butler.

"Willis, do me a quick favor. Contact Alice and Ricky. Tell them to meet me down in the bunker. Oh, and tell them it's urgent so they can go here faster."

"Right on it, Mr. Hawke."

Hawke smirked as he made his way down into the Nano-Bunker. He turned the lights on, revealing the already set of Nano Man armored exosuits sitting in a line against the wall. Hawke grinned.

"Good to see you all again." Hawke said to the Nano Man suits.

He sat down at the monitor, searching for any strange anomalies across the globe and discovers one up north around

Retropolis' cousin city, Mass City. Hawke nodded.

"Seems I have found Death herself."

From the bunker doors comes Alice and Ricky barging in, Hawke gazed up toward them with a large smile on his face. They look at him and are confused about what is going on.

"Why are we here, Nathan?!" Alice said.

"I need to speak with you."

"So, you had us rush over here just to talk to you?" Ricky said. "Seriously?"

"Um… yeah."

Alice grabbed a chair and sat next to Hawke. Ricky went over to the wall nearby and leaned against it, shaking his head. Alice gets into Hawke's face as he can see she's not happy about being rushed over just to have a word.

"Are you mad?" Hawke said. "You want some cake?"

"I don't want no damn cake! I hope this is important, Nathan. Because if it's not, you're going to be in trouble for this."

"It is important. So important that the earth as we know it is at stake."

Alice stared for a brief moment as Ricky cocked his head over, shocked look on his face as if he heard what he thinks he has heard.

"What?" Alice said.

"What do you mean the earth is at stake, Nate?" Ricky said. "What the hell is going on?"

"What are you not telling us?" Alice said. "What is it? Is it The Thetan again?

"No. It's beyond The Thetan. There're two individuals involved. Well, three from what has been given to us. Kex Kendrick, Death, and Noldar from some other realm or world."

"Kex Kendrick from KexInc.?!" Alice said. "Are you kidding me?!"

"No. This is not a joke."

"Who's Noldar?" Ricky said. "I've never heard of a Noldar before."

"He's a god from another realm of existence. They call him the Millennium god of guile."

"And who's Death?"

"Someone The Swordman wants gone from this world."

"Wait. Wait. Wait." Alice said shaking her head. "The Swordman?! There is no Swordman, Nathan. You know that."

Hawke looked at her with a confirmed look. He knows and from his look, Alice knows as well. The Swordman exists.

"We're scheduled to team up tonight for a mission. We have a tracking location to where Death and Noldar are located."

"I don't know what to say." Alice said. "I'm being completely honest here, Nathan."

"I'm lost for words." Ricky said. "Man, what is this world coming to when you have gods from other dimensions coming out and you have myths being confirmed as facts."

"A party." Hawke smirked. "It's the world we live in, guys. We just have to accept it as it is."

"As much as I don't want you going out there and risking your life, you know what to do."

"I think I do. I guess."

"This isn't a joke, Nathan. The Thetan almost killed you and your own business partner is trying to plot plans to kill you as he tried to kill us on the road."

"Wait, you're talking about Niles?"

"Yes."

"He tried to kill you?" Hawke said looking at Alice and Ricky. "Both of you?!"

"Brian too. Lucky for us, his driving skills came in handy."

Hawke sighed.

"After I finish with this mission stuff, I'll speak with Niles myself and put an end to all of his secret plotting."

Inside the Swordlair, Kenari sat down, staring at a monitor, showing a photo of Death and Noldar back at the T.I.T.A.N. Headquarters. From behind comes Allison Clark, Kenari's wife. She looked at the monitor, seeing Death.

"So, she's out there again?"

"She is."

"You intend to stop her don't you?"

"I have to, Allison. You know that. She can't be allowed to roam freely without someone watching her."

"I understand. I also understand this protocol thing you've gotten yourself into. I know you're doing it through the benevolence of your heart. I only want you to be careful."

"I know this. You don't have to repeat it to me every time before I go out there."

'Take me out there with you this time."

"You're not ready yet, Allison. You know that."

"I have been training for months with the Creed, Kenari. I need to go out in the field someday for the full experience."

"And someday you will. I'm not bringing you out there in the amount of chaos that will come during this. I love you too much to do that."

Allison nodded.

"I understand your caring. But, when the time is right, you know you'll have to take me out there with you."

Kenari walked over to her and kissed her, leaving the Swordlair.

Kenari walked into Clark Enterprises in Retropolis, going into the weapons room where his associates, Steven Cobb and Jacob Blake are waiting for him. Cobb and Blake are speaking with each other when they see Kenari approaching them from a distance.

"Good to see you once again, Mr. Clark." Steven said.

"Same here, sir." Blake said. "What can we do for you today?"

"I'm going out on an important mission and my suit needs

some upgrades."

"What kind of upgrades did you have in mind for the suit, sir?" Blake said.

"I need more plating. Enough to withstand an attack from a shotgun or two."

"Really?" Steven said. "You're going up against something that powerful, huh?"

"Appears to be the case of the matter. I need it to be much stronger than the current one."

Blake looked through the closet set of armors and nodded.

"I have just the thing for you, sir."

Blake presented the armor before Kenari, who placed his hand on it, feeling the texture of the material.

"This is one of the stronger ones, correct?"

"It is. Capable of withstanding blows from superhuman beings and high-powered weaponry."

"I'll take it."

"Very well, sir."

"Also, put some of the liquid solidium in it as well with a dash of radiation for protection."

Steven and Blake looked at Kenari strangely.

"Solidium and radiation? For what purpose would you need those, sir?"

Kenari looked at them with serious intent.

"Because this mission isn't the only problem I might be facing out there tonight."

"What's the other problem that would cause you to wear a suit of solidium armor laced with radiation?" Steven said.

"Because of Kex Kendrick's involvement in all of this, I have a firm feeling that the Chosen Son of Enigma City will be on our trail and from what I have heard, he's not a nice guy to get along with."

III

THE COLLISION OF HEROES

Kenari prepared himself inside the Swordlair, putting on the sword suit with its newly placed armor with solidium and radiation lacing. The armor was lean and with it, red glows of radiation emitted from the interior lines of the armor. Through the arms, legs, and body. Hawke as well is preparing himself in the exosuit of Nano Man, upgraded with a form of satellite tracking, able to track down certain criminals and locations within seconds. Flying out of his Nano-Bunker, he goes north, toward Retropolis. While flying there, he contacted The Swordman through his helmet communicator.

The Swordman jumped into the Sky-Rapier, which the residents call his Swordwing, as it hovered and flew out of the Swordlair with Allison watching him go. As he gets high into the air, he noticed Nano Man contacting him, he pressed a button on the sword wing panel, waiting for Nano Man to speak.

"I'm listening." The Swordman said.

"On this mission of ours, you have any idea where Death could be?"

"I have a lead on her somewhere in Mass City."

"I thought she would be trampling around Retropolis. Seemed like a city girl."

"No. She's beyond a city woman. Head to Mass City and meet

me there."

"We can't go in together like partners?"

"I'm closer to the city than you are."

"Eh, yeah. You're closer to the location. That's true. I'll see you there."

The Swordman hung up the call and flew past the Mass City entrance sign, where he later slowed the Swordwing down, searching the ground beneath him for any signs of disturbance. He overlooked the major parts of the small city, the financial area, neighborhood areas, shopping areas. Not finding Death anywhere. He turned the Swordwing around and noticed a pack of hooded figures running around in the street toward a small bar.

"Must be her pack." said The Swordman with confidence.

He landed the Swordwing on top of a nearby building, hidden from the sight of those on the ground. After exiting the flying vehicle, he could hear a roaring sound coming from above him, almost engine like but with a smooth sound following. The Swordman looked up and Nano Man landed in front of him.

"You made it I see." said The Swordman. "How fast were you going exactly?"

"Fast enough. I know it seems unreal for me to leave Jersey and enter Canada at such short notice. You know flying gets you to the location faster than driving, right."

"I am aware of that."

"Then, you're also aware that my suit is able to bypass any flying vehicle. Even your flying sword over here."

The Swordman looked down from the building, seeing the hooded figures entering the small bar, as if they were in a pack. Nano Man looked at Swordman's armor. Seeing the glowing red lining coming through it.

"What's with the extra armor this time around?"

"For a particular cause."

"I didn't expect Death to be someone of physical strength."

"It's not protection from her."

"Then who?"

"You'll see."

"When? I'm curious as to why its glowing red lines and why you're wearing it tonight. Its different than your usual attire."

"Enough with the trivia. We have to enter the bar down there."

"Why? You need a drink before going after Death?"

"She's in the bar."

"Oh. Could've said that and I wouldn't have made a drinking gesture."

The Swordman jumped down from the building, gliding to the ground with Nano Man following. Both land onto the street, facing the bar. Nano Man stared at the doors of the bar, waiting for them to open.

"So, how do we go about this?"

"What do you mean?"

"I mean, how do we enter the bar and get Death to follow our commands."

"We won't."

"You know her better than I do."

"True. I also know that we'll have to make her obey our commands."

The Swordman started walking toward the bar with Nano Man alongside him. They inched closer to the bar doors and as they approached them in about a inch of a foot, Nano Man stopped and raised his hands up, preparing to blow the doors down. The Swordman raised up his right hand and smacked Nano Man's arms down. He looked over to him.

"What are you doing?! I was about to blast the doors down."

"The doors don't need to be knocked down. They need to be kicked in."

The Swordman kicked in the bar doors, frightened those that

were sitting inside the bar. They both looked around as they walked into the bar, commanding the civilians inside to leave, for their lives depended on it. The Swordman looked toward the bar itself, seeing Death standing behind it, pouring drinks.

She looked up, seeing The Swordman and Nano Man as she gasped in joy.

"I see you've managed to find me. Both of you anyway."

"This game ends now, Death." said The Swordman.

"You're coming along with us for questioning." Nano Man said. "You got that?"

Death nodded, still pouring drinks.

"Mm-hmm. Yeah, I got you, Nanite."

Death stopped pouring the drinks and slid them across the bar. From the front doors, the side doors, and back doors arrived the hooded figures covered in black clothing with a black hood, detailed with skeletons and crosses on their attire, faces covered with a black shroud. They surrounded The Swordman and Nano Man. Death laughed at the sight of it. The Swordman was not very pleased. Nano Man was uncertain of what would take place at the moment.

"I see you have never met by Reapers before. How do they appeal to you guys?"

"Reapers, huh." Nano Man said. "Man, she's really into this whole 'Death' gig."

The Swordman counted the Reapers, measuring his current position and stance. He took a small gaze of the bar's surroundings. Nano Man's armor began to charge up, glowing a neon blue in the palm of his hands.

"What's the plan, Swords?"

"There's nine of them. Two of us."

"I don't get where you're going with this."

"Simple. Take out the ones on your side. I'll deal with the ones on mine. Are you ready?"

"Yeah. I'm ready."

The Swordman nodded, slowly reaching to his belt, pulling up a shuriken. He nodded to Nano Man as he threw the shuriken in the face of one of the Reapers, knocking him back as Swordman lunged toward him, punching him in the face and going after the other Reapers on his side. Nano Man started blasting energy beams at the reapers on his side, hovering up and slamming into their backs. One Reapers grabbed a stool and hit Nano Man in the back, having no effect due to the armor, Nano Man turned to the Reaper.

"You did notice this is armor, right?"

Nano Man head butted the Reaper, causing him to fall unconscious. Death smiled as she stood by and watched the entire brawl from behind the bar counter. She drank the drinks that she poured during the brawl. The Swordman delivered a series of blows to the Reapers from punches to kicks to knees in the heads to uppercuts that tossed the Reapers across tables. Nano Man continued fighting the Reapers on his end and fired a series of small missiles from his shoulders, eliminating and defeating the Reapers on his end.

"That about does it."

He looked over to The Swordman, who was facing his last Reaper. The Reaper tried to smash a pipe to Swordman's head, but Swordman grabbed the pipe, pummeled the Reaper with his fists and hit him in the back with the pipe. Dropping it next to him. He looked at Nano Man and nodded. Death started clapping with a smile on her face. Her black lipstick shining with the lights.

"You're coming with us, now." The Swordman said.

"Ugh. Fine." Death said, "Take me with you guys to wherever you're going."

Throwing the Swordman and Nano Man off their guards as Swordman placed death in handcuffs, taking her to the Swordwing. They walked out of the bar towards the building with the Swordwing on top. Nano Man looked to Death.

"You're even prettier up close."

"You want to get closer."

The Swordman jerked Death's arm. She grunted, liking The Swordman's force on her arm.

"Not too rough, Swords. It's still early."

He looked at Nano Man. Serious intention in his eyes.

"You're trying to put yourself in even more trouble?"

"No. No. It was just a compliment."

"For memory's sake, keep those kinds of complements away from her. Trust me, it will only do more harm than good."

The Swordman grappled up to the building with Death in tow, Nano Man flew up to the building as well. He watched as Swordman placed Death inside the Swordwing as he proceeded to enter as well.

"So, where are we taking her?"

"Nader said to bring her to the hoverbase for interrogation."

"What's the hoverbase?"

"You'll see. Make sure you look up when you do."

The Swordwing hovered and flew away with Nano Man flying behind him like a tail.

Up in the northern section of Canada, Commander Norland rides on his bike through the wilderness, doing a search for Kex Kendrick. Going through the forests and the mountains that are surrounding him, looking for any vehicles, buildings, or signs that may point to Kendrick. Norland finds none and signals out a call to Nader.

"Colonel. Nothing on Kendrick in this region."

"Understood. Proceed to the next region. Maybe you'll find something there."

"Yes sir."

Norland rode off out of the wilderness onto the nearby road that lead him west from the region.

Back at James' home, someone knocked on the door. Kent, who's sitting in the kitchen, hears it as James walked over to the door. Kent stood up, worried about his safety.

"James, be careful now."

"I will. I don't think no one is coming for you, Kent."

James opened the door, staring at Nader, who looked into the home, seeing Kent in the kitchen.

"Seems I've found the right place." Nader said. "May I come in, Mr. Porter?"

James turned and looked at Kent, waiting for an answer. Kent nodded and gestured his hand. James opened the door wider for Nader to enter in. Nader looked at Kent and greeted him.

"Don't worry, Mr. Brock, I'm not here to take you to General Lawler or the government."

"Then why are you here?"

"I'm here to tell you that we, T.I.T.A.N. need your assistance on something. Something big."

"You're referring to your little team you have set up?"

"I am. How did you know about it?"

"Trust me, Colonel, I know computers and I know tech just as much as radiation and weather patterns."

Nader nodded. "Well, that's good I guess."

"So, what do you want Kent to help you guys with?" said James. "I'm just curious as to what it could be."

"We need Mr. Brock to help us find two artifacts. Very ancient and both are surrounded with energy that e cannot explain. The energy is in a way close to radiation and that's why I came here to speak with Mr. Brock."

"You just need my knowledge to help you find two artifacts and that's it?"

"Yeah."

"So, you're not looking to use The Beast to your own gain?"

"No, we are not. We want to find these artifacts and that's it. We have our team our doing the fighting for us."

Kent looked at James and nodded to Nader. He approached him and the two shook hands.

"I will help you find the artifacts and that will be all I will do."

"Agreed. Your knowledge over the Beast is what we expect from you. Heard about your lab in Dallas. So, you'll have to come with me onto our new base of operations."

"And where is that?" James said.

"Right above your heads." Nader said pointing up as the sound of engines start to roar above them.

"What the hell is that?" Kent said.

"I hope it doesn't destroy my home." James said. "It's already been messed with."

They stepped outside of the home, looking up to the clear night sky, seeing a large object hovering above them. They were astonished at the sight and size of the object.

"What is that?" James said. "Is that a UFO?"

"No, not a UFO." Nader said. "It's called the hoverbase. Something that we're recently received with some financial aid from Mr. Hawke and Mr. Clark."

"I hope the laboratory doesn't have windows."

"It has maybe three to four. Nothing less than that."

From the hover base comes a hoverjet, lowering down to James' home, where Nader and Kent enter in. Nader looked at James.

"You want to come on board, Mr. Porter."

"No thanks, sir. I'll stay right here."

"Suit yourself."

"Keep me updated, Kent."

"I will."

The hoverjet hovered itself up into the air, reaching the height above the hover base, then lowering itself on top of the hover base. Where Nader and Kent exit and enter the interior of the hover base as it flew away from James' home. James shook his head.

"What you get yourself into, Kent. I will never fully understand."

Somewhere above the wilderness in the outskirts of Retropolis, the Swordwing flies across the sky with Nano Man keeping up. Nano Man contacts The Swordman once again as Swordman answered the call. Death looked at him with a faint smile on her face.

"Who's calling you?"

"None of your concern."

'I'm sure it about me anyhow. You guys can't stop talking about me can you."

"Keep quiet."

The Swordman answered Nano Man's call, still glaring at Death and piloting the plane.

"What is it?"

"Where's the hoverbase that you were talking about again?"

"It's close."

"You're sure about that? Because all I see around us is the clear night sky and the stars covering it."

"I am sure. It'll be here soon enough."

"If that's what you believe."

The radar on the Swordwing began to beep, Swordman looked at it and spotted an object coming straight for him and Nano Man. He recognizes the signature of the object. Its speed and its size.

"We have company coming." The Swordman noted. "Watch out."

"What are you talking about? Why would I have to--"

Nano Man is knocked across the sky, falling to the grounds of the wilderness. The Swordman spotted him falling, placing the Swordwing on autopilot, he opened the cockpit door. He looked back at Death, gazing at her handcuffs and seated position.

"You stay right where you are."

"Sure thing. I'm not going anywhere."

The Swordman jumped out of the Swordwing, down to the wilderness, where he landed onto the ground, surrounded by trees. He searched the area for Nano Man, looking for the glow of his armor through the darkness of the forest.

"Nano Man! Where are you?!"

Getting no response, The Swordman continued walking into the deep darkness and inside the Swordwing, Death sat, looking through the window down into the forest, able to see Nano Man's light in the forest with Swordman inching closer to him. She noticed something fly past the Swordwing and dive into the forest. She smiled.

"So, that's Kendrick little friend."

The Swordman kept walking and found Nano Man leaning against a tree, his armor damaged. Swordman walked over to him, checking to see if he's injured or not. Nano Man puts his hand up to Swordman.

"I'm alright." Nano Man said. "Just didn't expect that to happen."

"I'm aware of that."

Nano Man looked up into the air. "What the hell was that thing? The blow it gave me was powerful enough to damage my armor."

"I know what it was."

"What?"

Behind them, they hear something flying in the air. Both look and see the object coming down to the ground. The impact of its landing shook the trees around them. Nano Man slowly stood up from the tree as Swordman stared at the object.

"Is that who I think it is?" Nano Man said.

"Yeah. Its him."

The Swordman and Nano Man were staring at Taltus, The Powerman himself. Eyes shining gold as he stared at them. Death expressed a big smile on her face, seeing the three on the ground facing each other.

"Oh, the memories being made."

"So, that's why you have armor on." Nano Man said. "I get it now."

The Swordman stared deeply at The Powerman, while Nano Man was unprepared for what could happen next. While staring at Taltus, Nano Man received a call that came from Nader. Nano Man looked at Swordman.

"Nader, we're kind of in a situation right now."

"I'm sure you are, but there's another situation that's just come up."

"Which is?"

"Noldar has been spotted in New York City. Making demands for people to bow to him in Times Square. We need either you or Kenari to go after him."

"We're staring at The Powerman right now."

"The Powerman? There in front of the two of you?"

Nano Man gazed at Taltus, who stood boldly in front of him and The Swordman.

"Yeah."

"Very well, Hawke go to New York. Let Kenari deal with The Powerman."

"Seriously?"

"Yes. Kenari has prepared for that moment ever since he showed up. Now go to New York and stop Noldar."

"Must be why he's wearing the armor."

Nano Man hung up the call and looked at Swordman.

"I know it was Nader. Go stop Noldar."

"Wait, how did you know I was talking to Nader?"

"Because I can hear the conversations that Nader sends out through the hood."

"I see. You're sure you want me to leave you here with him?"

"Go. I've prepared for this moment. Stop Noldar and bring him in. I'll meet with you on the hover base."

"Gotcha."

Nano Man flew up into the air, out of the wilderness and passed the Swordwing, where Death looked at him, ashamed for him leaving.

"Oh, man."

The Swordman and The Powerman stared at each other. Taltus measured Swordman's stance. The Swordman's cloak flowed through the gust of the wind as did Taltus' cape.

"So, you're the mythological guy that's talked about up in these parts?"

"I am. I hear that you're talked about of being half-titan and half-god."

"Appears that both our questions are true."

"Why are you here?"

"I came here to stop you from your vigilantism. The world doesn't need men like you and that Nano Man. They need those like me. Who come out during the day and who don't wear masks of any kind."

The Swordman reached to his back and slowly pulled his sword up from its sheath. Prepared for a fight.

"You surely talk a lot for someone who isn't even a human. Banished from your birthplace, taken away from your parents. Hiding away in your fortress."

"How do you know---?"

"I study all who have come during my era. Such did you come in my era."

The Powerman hovered into the air above The Swordman. Who held his sword out toward Taltus.

"I've always wondered if that sword of yours is as powerful as the legends say."

"Come down here and find out."

The Powerman nodded as he flew toward The Swordman, going for a punch, but instead Swordman swipes Taltus' arm with the sword. The sword doesn't cut off his arm, but its powerful force knocked him to the ground. He looked up at Swordman, who pointed the sword down toward his neck.

"Stand up and face me like a man. Show me you are what they say you are."

The Powerman stood up and released a smile on his face. "Sure."

IV

<u>KNIGHT V. TITAGOD</u>

The Swordman and The Powerman duel it out in the wilderness of the night. Dodging blows and giving blows of their own. The Powerman went for another punch, but was unable to make a dent in the armor. Powerman looked at his fist.

"What kind of armor are you covered in?"

"Solidium armor with radiation lacing. Something that you're aware of."

The Swordman punched The Powerman several times and kicked him into a tree. Powerman took a second to regain his strength as Swordman ran toward him, kicking him through the tree. Powerman fell to the ground, he looked up and fired his lightning vision at Swordman, covering his suit, electrocuting him to an extent. Swordman shrugged off the lightning vision.

"I've heard about that maneuver of yours. Interesting how it comes from the eyes."

"It's internally charged then released. Something you didn't know apparently."

The Powerman swiftly moved toward The Swordman with speed, attacking him with a serious blow to the chest that knocked Swordman across the wilderness, through a pair of trees as well, leaving Swordman rolling on the dirt. Powerman flew toward him, but Swordman raised up his sword and smacked it across

Powerman's face, causing him to fly into a wall of a mountain.

"Mind your surroundings." The Swordman mentioned.

While the Swordman and The Powerman fighting it out with each other and Death overseeing it, Nano Man flies toward New York City, where Noldar is currently present, standing before a crowd of people in the middle of Times Square. At Times Square, Noldar, dressed in his green and brown war apparel with his ram-horned helmet, standing over citizens.

"I like the scenery here. All of you weak mortals, bowing your knee before me. Something that my kind will never understand nor do because of their ignorance to the truth."

Noldar looked around Times Square, gazing at the billboards, screens, and signs that surrounded the entire location as other citizens stood and watched from a distance. Noldar pointed toward them with his spear.

"Look at these mortals on the ground before me, peasants! You will soon do the same, but on a larger scale. The world as you know it, is soon to come to an end. Once it has ended, a new world will be built with me, Noldar, as your world's new and permanent king."

From the sky comes down Nano Man, armor still damaged as he faced Noldar. Noldar looked at him and his damaged armor. Nano Man held his hands up toward Noldar, prepared to fire a series of energy beams toward him.

"Let these people go, Noldar."

"You know of me." Noldar said. "My name is truly spreading across the lands of Eldigard."

"I don't know what an 'Eldigard' is. You're coming along with me for interrogation."

"Me? Interrogated by your kind? Is that what they told you to do?"

"Yeah. That's why I'm here. To stop you and to bring you in."

Noldar laughed as he circled around his spot.

"You mortals don't know what you're dealing with. I am a Millennium God. A new generation of gods that can and will overthrow the gods of old! I am Noldar, the Millennium God of Guile and I will not be stopped by some mortal in a metal suit of armor!"

"You want to test that boast?"

"I'm standing here, am I not."

Nano Man jolted back as he fired the energy beams at Noldar. The civilians run in horror away from the two battling it out in the streets of Times Square. Noldar goes for a swipe with his spear as Nano Man flew over him, punching him in the head and kneeing him in the back of his head. Noldar slowly starts to lose his patience.

"You think I'm an easy opponent?!"

Noldar fired a beam of energy from the spear, hitting Nano Man and knock him down onto the street. Noldar walked toward him and placed the end of the spear against his throat.

"You will kneel before me."

"Not really." Nano Man said, head-butting Noldar.

Nano Man and Noldar fight amongst themselves in Times Square, nearly destroying the buildings that surround them with civilians continuing to run away with horror from the location. Nano Man grabbed Noldar and flew up into the air, diving both himself and Noldar down through one of the buildings into the ground, covering the streets with debris and smoke.

In the western region of Northern Canada, Commander Norland stumbled upon an old factory building that belongs to Kendrick. He gets off his bike and enters into the factory. Inside the base, Norland noticed it's still in safe conditioning and finds

Kendrick standing on one of the rooms. Norland stood behind him in a distance.

"Kex Kendrick." Norland said. "Stop what you're doing here."

Kendrick turned around, seeing Norland. He clapped and smiled at him. Gesturing to his white and red military uniform.

"Commander Norland in the flesh." Kendrick said. "I've always wondered how you look in person and now I have the answer."

"We know you're in alliance with Death and Noldar, Kendrick. I'm taking you with me for questioning."

"Taking me where?"

"You're coming with me. As of right now."

"I think not, Northern Defender. I'm staying right where I am until I finish my work here."

From behind Kendrick appear the Exchange Force, ready and prepared to combat Commander Norland. Norland stared at the Force and looked toward Kendrick, who continued to smirk with arrogance.

"You're not going to fight your own battle, huh?"

"I believe the Exchange Force can answer that question for you, Commander Norland."

Kex turned around back to his business and signaled the Force to attack and kill Norland. The Force ran toward Norland, who fought the four of them at once. Kicking and punching them as close as they could possibly get. Kendrick stood by and watched the battle go on. The Force later was able to get Norland on the ground, pummeling him in his back and kicking him in his sides.

"He's not as tough as ADDER proclaims." One of the Force said.

"Now, kill him." Kendrick said. "Do it quickly and I'll pay you all double the previous cost."

The Force goes to stab Norland in his back with their swords, but Norland releases a small wave of lighting around them, freezing them and electrocuting them where they stood. Norland instantly took the Exchange Force out with a series of blows to the head and kicks to the abdomens. As the Four were being defeated, Kex ran out of the factory with Norland chasing him to the outside. Norland reached the outside of the factory, seeing Kex driving in a jeep away from the location. Norland jumped onto his bike and chased down Kendrick's jeep. Driving through the snow as it begins to grow inch by inch on the ground, Norland pulled out his gun and starting shooting at the jeep's tires. The shots hit the back tire as Kendrick noticed it.

"Son of a bitch!"

Kendrick pressed a button inside the jeep, causing it to release small grenades from the trunk. Norland spotted the grenades as they exploded, causing a miniature landslide, covering the roadway between him and Kendrick. Norland sighed.

"You have to be joking me right now."

Nano Man and Noldar continue their brawl in Times Square with Nano Man firing continuous shots of energy at Noldar, knocking him to his knees. Noldar fired a set of beams from his spear at Nano Man, who seemly blocked them with his own beams firing back at them.

"We've been playing this game long enough, Noldar."

"This is not a game, mortal! This is the beginning of my ruler ship."

"Uh… ok."

Nano Man stood back and from his chest fired the ultra-beam at Noldar, jolting him into a wall, almost knocked out, but out of energy to possibly fight back. Noldar took some breathes while Nano Man walked over to him. Looking down at Noldar, kicking his spear to the side. Noldar smirked, wiping the sweat from his forehead and the blood from his mouth.

"You think you've won?! You haven't even reached the surface."

"I've put you down. So, that's a start."

Thunder rumbled over New York City. Noldar instantly looked up toward the lightning that flashed from the coming clouds. Nano Man also gazed up, seeing the clouds coming from out of nowhere. He turned to Noldar, seeing him shivering and crouching closer to the wall.

"Scared of a small thunderstorm?"

"I don't mind the thunderstorm. I'm just not fond of the one who creates them."

"That's unfortunate."

Nano Man looked around and from the sky, a lightning bolt crashed into the streets of Times Square. Noldar hid behind the wall as he knew what had just come down from the clouds. Nano Man approached the site, seeing a man crouched down in the street, wearing black and silver armor with a silver helmet accompanied with wings and is holding a silver and black war hammer.

"I don't know who you are, but I suggest you stand up and tell me your name?"

The man stood up, staring at Nano Man. He looked over and seen Noldar crouched over behind the wall. The man turned his attention back to Nano Man.

"I am Theus. The Son of Eden and Prince of Eragard."

"I've never heard of you. Must be from the same place as Noldar I take it."

"Move out of my way."

"Why would I do that? It seems to me that you and Noldar are in cahoots with one another. Are the two of you allies?"

"We are not allies. We are enemies. I'm taking him back to Eragard for the crimes that he has committed across the realms of the universe."

"The universe, huh. If you don't mind, hammer man, I'm taking him in for questioning at my own place of justice."

"I think not, machine."

"I think so."

Theus smirked, looking around Times Square, holding his war hammer tightly. Nano Man turned away from Theus, going toward Noldar. Theus threw his war hammer at Nano Man, he turned around as the hammer was driven into his chest, pushing him through a window of a building. Noldar looked and stared at Theus, who was approaching him.

"What are you doing, Son of Eden?!"

"I'm taking you to Eragard. Justice will send you to your eternal prison."

The hammer returned to Theus as he began to hover up in the air with Noldar in tow. Nano Man walked out of the crashed window, looking up and seeing Theus hovering and preparing to fly away with Noldar.

"Hell no."

Nano Man flew toward Theus and kicked him across the street. Theus fell to the ground, still holding the hammer. Nano Man took his stance in front of Theus with Noldar behind him.

"You think you can overcome me, machine?!"

"I can try."

"Try you shall and fail you will."

Nano Man and Theus flew toward each other. Crashing into one another as they flew up the side of a building, knocking each other into the billboards and screens around Times Square. Nano Man punched Theus and grabbed his cape, twisting him in the air before throwing him into another billboard.

"Where do all of you guys come from?"

Theus hovered into the air and grabbed Nano Man by his throat. Punching him from his head to his abdomen. Nano Man snatch Theus by his throat and delivered blows of his own with an uppercut last, knocking Theus to the ground. Nano Man flew down toward Theus and stomped him in his chest. Theus laughed the attack off.

"You are very powerful, machine. But I am no ordinary being."

Theus grabbed Nano Man's foot and held him up in the air, slamming him into the pavement of the street and tossed him against a wall, cracking it from the strength of Theus' power. Nano Man realizes his armor won't hold up much longer as he runs to Theus, punching and kicking him.

He fires another series of energy beams at Theus, but they have no effect as Theus raised up his hammer and smacked Nano Man in the head, the force of the hammer caused Nano Man to fly across the road, slamming him through a series of buildings.

"I've dealt with your little game long enough, machine."

"You showed him your power, Son of Eden." said Noldar. "Just leave me be for now. I'll make my return to Eragard in no time."

"No. No you will not, Millennium God of Guile."

Theus grabbed Noldar as Nano Man was slowly coming from the building he crashed into. Theus looked at Nano Man and flew up into the air with Noldar holding onto him. Nano Man stared at Theus and Noldar in the air.

"I'm not giving up."

Nano Man flew up into the air, behind Theus and chasing him with quick speed.

"You're not taking away my prisoner."

The Swordman and The Powerman continue to fight as Swordman tries to tell him that he is not the primary enemy. Powerman doesn't want to hear his words as Swordman kicked him in the chest and elbowed him in the head.

"You just listen to me for once!"

"No."

"I am not your enemy! Nano Man is not your enemy! The enemy is who we're after. There's a planetary threat coming, and you need to listen to me."

"Don't try to save yourself with talking."

"I'm not trying to save me. I'm trying to save you."

The Powerman lunged toward The Swordman and again he swiped the sword against him, but Powerman grabbed the sword, snatched it away from Swordman, throwing it across the forest. Powerman grabbed Swordman by the throat and held him up. Death watched on with a smile continually.

"This fight is about to get good!" Death smiled. "Get it going!"

The Swordman started kicking The Powerman in the chest and ribs to break the hold on his neck. The attacks do not faze him as he held Swordman's throat tightly, slowly squeezing his throat, attempting to suffocate him in his hand. Swordman slowly reach to his belt, pulling out a small object.

"Your days of vigilantism are over with."

"Not until my appointed time has come."

The Swordman tossed the object into The Powerman's face. He released the hold on Swordman, backing away from eh object. He gazed at the object, seeing it's a small container filled with red radiation.

"Where did you get that from?"

"I… have my sources…"

The Swordman walked over toward the trees, retrieving his sword as he walked toward The Powerman, standing over him as he slowly tried to regain his strength. Swordman raised up the sword above Powerman's neck.

"The people of Enigma City call you their 'Chosen Son'." The Swordman mentioned. "That makes me wonder what they would call you if you were on the other side of the law."

"Like you? They believe you're only a myth. A legendary tale told by their ancestors throughout time."

"I am."

The Swordman was prepared to eliminate The Powerman from his life.

"I will say this again, Taltus. I am not your enemy. What I am about to do will prove that to you."

The Swordman was set to execute The Powerman, suddenly a loud bang was sounded from the sky. The Swordman looked up and noticed three objects in the sky that were heading in his direction. He looked closer and its Nano Man latched into Theus' back with Noldar holding onto Theus' leg. Nano Man elbowed Theus in the head and punched him in his back, causing him to fall to the ground in front of Swordman and Powerman. On the ground, Noldar looked around seeing The Swordman, The Powerman, Nano Man, and Theus all starting to face each other. He took several steps back and looked up at the Swordwing, seeing Death inside. She looked down at him, making gestures to come and get her from the plane.

The Swordman, The Powerman, and Nano Man stood up as Theus stood to his feet. Theus looked and saw the three of them.

"You have allies, machine."

"I have one over here. The other one I'm not aware of."

"The Powerman will be fine. It seems we have another one to deal with, huh?"

"This guy said he's come to take Noldar to Eldigard or Eragard."

"I know of the realm."

Theus turned and looked at The Powerman. Noticing his armored uniform and sensing an unusual energy from him and recognizing the aura that came along with it.

"You're one of them. One of those of a titagod."

"I am the only titagod." Taltus proclaimed. "There is no other."

Theus threw the hammer at Powerman, slamming him into a tree. Nano Man fired shots of energy beams at Theus, while The Swordman stood by and watched the battle unfold with his sword clenched in his right hand. Theus swiftly flew over to Nano Man, smacking him in the chest with his hammer, the attack rolled Nano Man around the ground as he collided into a trunk. Theus turned to Swordman. Both with weapons of their own.

"That sword. I sense a power from it. An ancient power."

"There is an ancient power here. I recommend you do not test it."

"I am the Millennium God of Thunder. Nothing can withstand my power!"

Theus jumped up in the air above The Swordman, coming down with the hammer about to crash onto him. Swordman raised up his sword and swiped it toward Theus' hammer. The two powerful weapons collided, creating a large shockwave of energy that flowed from the collision, destroying the trees and mountain that stood nearby. The wave's great force knocked Theus to the ground. After the wave had disappeared, nothing was left standing around them except The Swordman, who held the sword above him. The Powerman, Nano Man, and Theus stood up, looking at one another and Swordman.

"Are we finished up here?" The Swordman said.

"I think we are." Nano Man said.

Swordman placed Noldar inside the Swordwing behind Death. They looked at one another with smiles.

"Nice to see you, Noldar."

"Same I say to you, Death."

"The two of you should keep quiet." The Swordman said. "I will rather not here your little conversations."

The Powerman approached Swordman as Theus did as well.

"I sense something in you that I didn't see at first." The Powerman said.

"Because you were blinded to what you could see." said The Swordman. "I know these things very well.

"You're taking Noldar to your base of operations?" Theus said. "For an interrogation?"

"I am."

"I will be coming along with you." said Theus. "To oversee Noldar's actions of course."

"I can agree with that."

"So will I." The Powerman said. "I will learn what this threat is you've spoken of."

Nano Man looked at his armor, completely damaged and in need of full repair round.

"I'm going to need another suit of armor. Thanks to you overpowered guys."

"Your suit has made an impression on me." The Powerman said. "The same can be said about The Swordman's."

"I never knew a machine could have such honor." said Theus. "Its an impressive accomplishment."

Nano Man's helmet opened up, revealing Hawke's face.

"I'm not a machine, Thunder God. I'm a man. A man in a suit you can say."

Theus nodded.

"Never encountered such feats of possibilities in my time."

"You're learn much more than you know. Swordman said.

"I'm prepared to do so."

"Make sure the three of you can keep up." The Swordman said as he entered the Swordwing.

The Swordman nodded as he flew away in the Swordwing with The Powerman, Nano Man, and Theus behind him.

V

INTERROGATING ONE'S DEATH

The Swordwing flew across the night sky with The Powerman, Nano Man, and Theus flying behind him. They fly over the mountains and forest beneath them. In front of them, The Swordman spotted a large object hovering in the air behind a small set of clouds.

"There's our base." The Swordman said. "Prepare yourselves for landing."

The hoverbase sat still in the air as they appeared before it. Landing on top of the hoverbase, T.I.T.A.N. agents come out of the doors, apprehending Death and Noldar from the Swordwing. Taltus, Nano Man, and Theus land atop the hoverbase, looking around at the amount of hover jets that sat on top of it.

"So, this is where my money has gone." Nano Man said. "I like it."

"You aided in creating this colossal vessel?" Theus said.

"I gave in some input of course. Wasn't just me that gave assistance into creating it."

"Best we head inside." said The Swordman.

They headed into the interior of the hover base, following the agents with Death and Noldar in their possession. While walking inside the hover base, they get a look around the base, seeing offices, laboratories, and control rooms all around them. From the

217

corner on the left walked Commander Norland. He spotted Swordman and Nano Man in the middle of the room.

"Look who's come in to join us." Norland said.

"Appears you made it before we did." said The Swordman. "How did the search for Kendrick go?"

"Kendrick?" The Powerman said. "He's involved with this?"

"He is. I tracked him down to one of his factories up north. He released some group called the Exchange Force on me. I defeated them and chased him out of the factory and into the woods, where I lost him after he released a set of grenades, creating a landslide. Which blocked me from chasing him any further. So I returned here in hopes of finding more information to where he may be."

"I will assist you on your mission to find Kex Kendrick. Trust me, it will be my honor."

"I'm all right with that."

"What will you do with Noldar?" Theus said. "When will he be put up for his judgment?"

"After we interrogate him." The Swordman said. "But, firstly, Death will be the one interrogated."

Nader walked up a set of stairs, passing by crowds of agents to approach the team. They noticed him coming toward them, standing their ground as Death and Noldar were being walked down a hallway toward their cells. Noldar looked toward one lab and inside of it was Kent Brock, studying the artifacts, which they retrieved from Noldar while entering the interior of the base. Noldar stared at Brock and nodded toward him with a sinister smirk on his face, intimidating Brock for as second.

"You brought them in I see." Nader said. "Job well done."

"When will it be time for interrogation?" The Swordman said. "I would like to start immediately."

"Give them some minor time inside their cells. Make them feel secluded from the rest of the world around them. You can interrogate her afterwards.”

Nader looked, seeing Taltus and Theus standing behind The Swordman and next to Nano Man and Commander Norland.

“I know of you. The Powerman from Enigma City. Their Chosen Son and savior.”

“Call me Taltus and I am not their savior.”

Nader stared at Theus. Seeing how he’s dressed in what appeared to be a mixture of medieval and advanced clothing.

“What of you? You seem too be from a different world than ours? I take it you’re from the world where Noldar is from.”

“I am Theus, Millennium God of Thunder and Prince of Eragard. I have come to bring Noldar to justice for the crimes he has committed across the realms.”

“I knew it.”

The T.I.T.A.N. agents placed Death in one cell and Noldar in another. They are a few feet of distance from each other but are able to hear each other’s voice if spoken loudly. Death giggled and clapped inside of her cell, while Noldar say quietly, spending time inside of his mind.

“We’re inside!” Death said. “Noldar, we’re inside!”

“I know we are, Death. I can see that.”

“It’s amazing. Don’t you think so?”

“No. I do not think it is a pleasure to be trapped behind a cell once again. I’ve shared my time behind bars.”

“Me too. But that doesn’t stop me from cheering myself up with a clever plan of escaping.”

Noldar turned his head to the wall, interested in Death’s choice of words.

“What is your plan of escape, exactly?”

“It’s simple. Get out of this cell of course.”

“You’re not escaping the base itself.”

“Oh, I am. There are ways that we can.”

“Take these moments of yours to plan your escape, Death. I

will be busy contacting someone outside of these metallic walls."

"Oh. Telepathy. I like it."

Noldar shook his head and closed his eyes. Going inside of his mind to find the one he wants to speak with.

Nader walked down the hallway, passing by Noldar's cell, seeing him inside with his eyes closed, as if he's meditating.

"I didn't know you like to meditate."

"I'm not meditating, Colonel. I'm communicating."

Nader nodded. "Yeah right."

Nader approached Death's cell with a few agents to his side. The agents opened the door as Death gazed at them.

"This some group thing you guys have an interest in?"

"We're taking you to the interrogation room." Nader said. "We need answers about your plans with the artifacts. You have the answers."

"I'm sure you think I do."

The agents grabbed Death by her arms, walking her out of the cell and down the hallway. Passing by Noldar's cell, Death looked over toward it, seeing Noldar sitting down.

"Guess I'm first, Noldar!"

Noldar stayed quiet, sitting down. The agents walked past him as did Nader.

They took Death into the interrogation room, which resembled a room similar to the ones inside police departments with the one table and mirror window. They sit Death down in the chair and exit the room, while Nader entered and stood by the door.

Death was handcuffed to the table. She looked at her handcuffs, rubbing them with her fingers.

"Have you used these handcuffs on someone else before?" Death said. "Because I'm picking up a particular sense of usage here."

"You're not here about the damn handcuffs." Nader said. "Tell us what you know about the artifacts you and Noldar took from us at our headquarters."

"The artifacts. The artifacts. Oh! Yeah. I remember them. We needed them to execute our plan as quickly as possible."

"What do you mean as quick as possible?"

"You know. We were in a major hurry. Like we are right now to get our plans done."

"For what purpose?"

"I'm not telling you the purpose of our plans."

"Why won't you tell me?"

"Because, you're just a ordinary man who is in charge of a secret intelligence organization. You know nothing about the mystical or supernatural that has roamed the earth for eons."

"You know, you're right about that, Death." Nader said. "I don't know a lot about the mystical and supernatural. But, I know someone who does."

Nader opened the room door and in came The Swordman. Staring hard at Death. He walked over toward the table and sat down in front of her as she smiled toward him. Her cheeks beginning to blush.

"This isn't a good time to smile." The Swordman said.

"It is for me. You're sitting right in front of me. Its beautiful!"

"I suggest you tell us about what you know of the artifacts and what they can do with their power."

"Well, the artifacts have power. Both of them. You need to know how to tap into that power in order to understand it or control it to your liking."

"Tell us your plan for the artifacts. The truth. No lies."

"No lying. Ok. I intend to use the artifacts to release my brother from his imprisonment."

"Your brother?!" Nader said. "Seriously, she has a brother?!"

"I know the history concerning the artifact and your supposed brother. Truthfully, I wouldn't release him from his prison after the things he has done in this world."

"That's because you don't know him like I do, Swords. If you knew him like I do and understood what his true motives are for the world and this cosmos, you would do the same thing that I intend to do and that is release him from his prison. He doesn't belong in there."

"What he did in the past, to those people, to those lands, he deserves to remain in his imprisonment for all eternity."

"See, you're blind like the rest of these common folks around here. I thought you would have some sort of understanding. I thought you would aid us in bringing him back into this world. It seems to me that you're just as weak and as blind as the world itself already is."

The Swordman snatched Death's coat, pulling her closer to the table and to himself. She giggled from the pull as Nader slowly reached down to his side for his gun.

"Calm down, Swordman." said Nader. "We don't need you killing her just yet."

"Not until she gives us what we need."

"So much testosterone in you. Ha! Funny."

"Tell us why you assisted with Noldar and Kex Kendrick in this little scheme of yours."

"Um. I needed some partners to do this whole thing with. So, Noldar, being the Millennium God that he is, was able to open portals across the universe and he knows much about the artifacts. Kendrick on the other hand was our assistant operator in our plans. Mainly for destinations and secret bases."

"I'm taking you back to Pegasus Prison. You understand me?"

"Yeah. Yeah. I got you, Swords. Never can get enough of me can you."

"This isn't a game."

"It is for me. Everything is simply a game. Life itself is the greatest game."

Noldar sat in his cell, mentally communicating with Kex Kendrick across distant miles from the air to the ground. Kendrick sat inside an office of one of his homes in the country lands.

"Kex Kendrick, do not be afraid. This is Noldar speaking with you."

"Noldar. Where are you?"

"I'm currently occupied inside a flying base behind bars."

"What?"

"You heard what I said. There's currently interrogating Death and I am next."

"This isn't good. This isn't good at all. What do you need me to do for the two of you to escape?"

"Death said she had a plan."

"What plan could she possibly have."

"I do not know. But, when they brought me inside of this fortress, I seen a man that is known for something living within him."

"Who are you talking about?"

"A man named Kent Brock I hear."

"I've never heard of the man before in my life."

"Well, you're going to hear about him now because he's the heroes' upcoming threat."

"How do you know of this?"

"Because inside Kent Brock lays a powerful and sleeping Beast. Once I awake it, it will come out and cause mayhem for all on this vessel. When that happens, I will make my escape route out of here."

"Do what you must to escape. Because our plan needs to be activated soon."

"I understand."

Noldar opened his eyes, disconnecting from Kendrick and

staring at a number of agents who are staring at him through the door. He smiled at them and waved.

"Did you enjoy watching me talk to myself?"

"Not really." said a group of agents, walking away from Noldar's cell.

The Swordman continued to interrogate Death as Nader watched on. Concerned about his well-being as well as Swordman's rising temper. Death continued to giggle and laugh while being pulled and shoved by The Swordman.

"Either you tell us everything or die where you're sitting."

"How can I die? I'm Death."

The Swordman shoved Death to her chair and pulled his sword out and placed it to Death's throat. Nader unaware of Swordman's actions, tried to calm him down and persuade him to remove the sword from Death's throat. Declining to remove it, he pressed it against Death's throat as she coordinated to laugh.

"You're about to do it aren't you?!"

"I won't hesitate to do it." said The Swordman. "Give us what we need, and I'll remove the sword from your neck."

"Aw, what the hell. Ok. Ok. I'll tell you. We planned to go to Retropolis to break the artifact open and release my brother. That is the true plan. I swear to you."

"Is that right?"

"It is. That is our plan. To release my brother from his prison, so he may destroy this world and rule it afterwards."

"You can remove the sword." Nader said. "She gave us the location of their plan."

"I know that."

"Put down the sword."

The Swordman stared at Nader, slowly removing the sword from Death's throat. He placed the sword back into its sheath and walked out of the interrogation room. Death sat down, with her head down, laughing quietly.

"Everything a damn joke to you?" Nader said. "He was about to kill you."

"Did you know that laughter is also a cause of death? I do. That's why I laugh."

"You're one crazy woman."

Nader exited the interrogation room with Death still handcuffed inside. He walked down the hallway, seeing Swordman in the distance, going to the top of the hoverbase. Nader ran after him.

"Swordman! Where are you going?!"

"I'm going to Retropolis to find out what their real plan is. She didn't tell us the truth."

"How do you know that?"

"Because I know her."

The Swordman paused and looked at Nader. Concerning showing on his face.

"You didn't leave her in there by herself, did you?"

"She's handcuffed to the table. What can she possibly do?"

The Swordman left from the stairs and ran back down the hallway toward the interrogation room. Nader ran after him.

In the interrogation room, Death slipped out a small chain from her coat sleeve, using it to cut the handcuffs from the table. Doing so, she escaped from the interrogation room and ran down the hallway to Noldar's cell. One guard stood watch as she approached him and stabbed him in his chest with one of her death crosses. Taking the keys from his belt, she opened the door to Noldar's cell. Inside, Noldar looked at her as the door opened. He smiled.

"Come on. Let's get out of here." Death said.

'Surely.'

They leave the cell hallway, walking through the halls,

surpassing the agents that are running toward the interrogation room as the alarm was sounded. Noldar looked and spotted Brock inside the lab.

"Wait, we need him for our plan."

"Um… why?"

"Because, what lies in him will be our primary weapon."

Death thought for a moment. She realized what Noldar was talking about and smiled.

"I like it."

Noldar waved his hand in the air, creating a mist of green aura. He commanded it to flow into the lab and toward the head of Brock. The mist made its way into the lab through an air vent and surrounded Brock's head as he was studying the two artifacts. Brock later stopped in his tracks and stood still, knowing something was wrong with him. Noldar laughed.

"Sorry to bother you at this moment of time, but I need your fellow friend who lives inside."

Brock tried to fight off Noldar's aura but was unable to succeed as it surrounded his head, causing him to trip and fall to the ground, hitting his head against a table.

"Here he comes." Noldar said. "Our weapon of destruction."

Brock started to shake and shiver on the ground, while Death ran into the lab, taking the two artifacts, Noldar miniaturized them as Death put them inside her coat pocket.

"How do we get outside of this thing?" Death said.

"Like this."

Noldar waved his hand again, only this time he created a portal, where he and Death walked through it, leaving the hoverbase. As they were walking through the portal, Norland spotted them and immediately ran after the two.

"No, you don't!" Norland said.

He ran toward them as Noldar turned around and gave him a smirk before closing the portal. Norland stopped running as the portal had disappeared into thin air. Norland looked around for anything he could find. Finding nothing and noticing the artifacts were gone.

"Damn it!"

Norland pulled out his radio, contacting Nader and the others to come to his location. After several seconds, they come and notice Kent shivering on the ground and the artifacts missing.

"What in the hell happened here?" Nader said.

"Death and Noldar escaped through some kind of wormhole." Norland said. "They must've attacked Brock and took the artifacts with them. The wormhole closed as I was trying to reach them."

They tried to help Kent up to his feet, but he fought back against them. Realizing that his strength was increasing, and his anger was rising, the team took several steps back from him.

"He's about to transform." The Swordman said.

"Transform?" The Powerman asked. "Transform into what?"

Kent tossed the lab table up in the air as the team continued to take steps back. The Swordman pulled out his sword as Nano Man prepared his energy beams. Nader pulled out his gun, while Theus and Taltus set their stance.

"Whatever is wrong with this man here, we will make sure he brings no harm to anyone." Theus said.

The Swordman looked at Kent and turned to The Powerman, testing his knowledge of the matters throughout the world.

"You've heard about the Beast who roamed through the northern Canadian forests?"

"I know of the accounts?"

"Then prepare yourself to witness it first-hand."

Kent screamed as his skin started falling off his body like shreds of paper, the dark gray hair arose from underneath the shredded skin, shoving it from his body as his eyes turned to a dark red and his hair increased in its growth of length, turning black. Kent's body changed shape and his height increased.

"This is what I feared the most of what would happen." Nader said.

"The fear is here, Colonel." The Swordman said. "We must settle him."

Kent turned around slowly, facing the team head on. They know it isn't Kent anymore. it's The Unstoppable Beast, who roared at them and is angry to the core of his being.

Inside of the Beast's head is Noldar's voice, using mind control to have possession over him. The Beast will respond and command anything that Noldar tells him to do. Noldar is able to see through the Beast's own two eyes. He sees the team in front of him.

"My Beast." Noldar said. "Destroy them."

The Beast roared as he lunged toward the team, causing destruction inside the hoverbase. Creating holes in its side from the attacks between the Beast and the team.

"We have to take this fight to the outside!" The Swordman said.

The team stepped back, opening one of the hover base's doors, leading the Beast to jump to the outside with the team following him down toward the ground.

"I didn't expect us to be doing this!" Norland said.

"Believe me, it was meant to come." The Swordman said. "We must make sure he doesn't harm any innocents down there."

Nader looked outside of the door, seeing the team following The Beast down toward the small country town. Nader shook his head.

"Bringing him on board is my mistake." Nader said. "I'm going to pay for that with my life."

The Beast and the team land to the ground, with The Beast charging toward them as they dodged his attack. The Beast swiped The Swordman and Nano Man across the open field as The Powerman flew toward him with a punch, but The Beast grabbed

Powerman's fist and slammed him into the dirt. Norland jumped onto the Beast's back, striking him with small lightning bolts in his punches. The Beast roared, he fell to his back with Norland still handing on as Theus dove toward him, smashing him what the hammer to his face.

"This monster isn't as strong as he appears." Theus said.

The Beast stared at Theus and punched him into the ground. Roaring at the team. The Swordman got to his feet, with Nano Man standing next to him.

"He's stronger than he looks." Nano Man said.

"Don't be so sure on appearances." The Swordman said. "They can deceive you."

"What are we going to do about him, Kenari?"

"Whatever it takes."

VI

<u>THE RAGE OF A BEAST</u>

The Swordman leads the team in the middle of a small country town against The Unstoppable Beast, of which they are unaware is being controlled in the mind by Noldar, who along with Death have teleported to one of Kex Kendrick's base of operations. The Beast roared at the team once more.

"We need a plan." The Swordman said.

"Got any ideas in your mind?" Nano Man said. "I'm just curious to see what you have in mind for this monster."

"I have a few things that could work. But, they'll have to listen to me."

"I don't see how that would be a problem."

The Beast roared as Theus was flying toward him with the hammer in front. Theus slammed the hammer against the left arm of The Beast. Who turned and faced him, anger in his eyes as he grabbed Theus' arm, holding the hammer and throwing him into a nearby barn.

"Norland, Powerman, Theus. I need you to listen." said The Swordman.

"What is it?" Norland said. "You have a plan?"

"I do. But we'll have to work together on this."

"I'm in." The Powerman said.

"How do we stop this brute creature?" Theus said.

"Powerman and Theus will take him head on. Nano Man, you'll take him from the air. Norland and I will take him from all sides. We have to weaken him down before we can tell if he's near defeat. If not, we must keep combating him until he tires out."

"Wait. He can tire out?"

"He's only a monster. His stamina won't last long after fighting those who's power level is near his own. I've done the research to know this."

"You're always prepared for this like this, Swordman?" said The Powerman.

"I'm prepared for all things."

The team stood in front of The Beast, who walked toward them, heavily breathing like a wild animal. His dark gray hair and red eyes stood out from anything else on him. The team took their stance, ready for the fight.

"You're sure this is going to work?" Norland said.

"It will."

The Beast roared loudly, stomping his foot into the roadway. The Swordman signals them to attack The Beast. The Powerman and Theus fly straight toward Beast, ramming him with punches and hammer smashes. Shoving him back near the trees. Nano Man flew above the battle, blasting Beast with his energy beams. The Beast roared in pain from the triple attacks he was received. The Swordman nodded toward Norland who closed his eyes and caused a series of lightning bolts to strike down on Beast, freezing him somewhat.

"I'm not sure my beams are working on him!" Nano Man said.

"Keep firing them." said The Swordman. "If they don't succeed, go for your other one."

"Right on it."

The Powerman rammed into The Beast's abdomen, picking him up and slamming him into the ground, which Powerman dodged over as Theus crashed down on Beast with his hammer and boot, colliding onto The Beast's chest and face.

"This monster is almost out of his course." Theus said. "He's no match for us!"

The Beast grabbed Theus and Powerman by their capes and slammed them continuously into the road, creating potholes with their bodies. Norland released another lightning bolt onto Beast, but the freezing didn't occur this time as The Beast's hairy body has melted the ice before it began to freeze onto his body and the lightning appeared to increase his strength.

"I should've known." The Swordman said. "The lightning."

"What of the lightning?" Norland said. "It's not working it seems."

"It is working. But, not to our advantage. Making him stronger."

Nano Man took a look at Beast closer through his helmet and noticed a strange energy of aura surrounding The Beast's head. Unknown to what the aura could be, it concerned Nano Man and could give him a clue to something else going on with Beast.

"There's some strange energy surrounding his head."

"What kind of energy?" The Swordman said.

"I'm not sure. Almost similar to Theus' energy and his hammer."

"He's being mind-controlled."

"I'm still going to blast him though. For our protection at least."

Nano Man charged his armor up, releasing the ultra-beam from his chest. The ultra-beam falls down onto The Beast, he roared as he looked up toward Nano Man. The Beast jumped up into the air and snatched Nano Man by his leg, pulling him down to the road, where The Beast began to pummel Nano Man's armor, simply destroying it.

"I got him." Norland said as he speared The Beast away from

Nano Man.

Nano Man laid on the ground, unable to move as his suit was completely damaged and unresponsive to his commands. The Swordman walked over to Nano Man, seeing his armor exosuit.

"I know. I'm screwed."

"Not just yet."

In a secret location, Death, Noldar, and Kendrick sat around the two artifacts. Noldar sat in an area alone, watching the Beast battle the team through his eyes. Death stared at him as if she was watching a TV. Kendrick sat and only stared at the artifacts on the table.

"What's going on now, Noldar?" Death said.

"The Beast is doing what I intended it to do."

"No fair you get to watch the whole thing."

"Can we focus a little on these artifacts here. I want to know which one possesses this Dark God I keep hearing about."

"Oh." said Death. "That would be this one right here."

She pointed to the Holy Artifact of Life and tapped it. Kendrick stood up above it, rubbing his hand across it. Smiling to himself.

"How do we get him out of there?"

"First off, we can speak to him directly."

"How is that even possible?" Noldar said. "I thought he was imprisoned on the inside."

"He is. But, he can still hear all that is around this artifact. He's heard everything."

Death placed the Holy Artifact of Life atop the mystical artifact. Both began to glow different shades of colors with the Holy Artifact of Life, glowing brighter than the other. Kendrick stood back along with Noldar, who crouched almost underneath the table in the corner. Death walked up to the table, her eyes locked on the artifacts. She showed off a big smile.

"It's working! It's working! It's working!"

The artifacts slowly turned from a shade of colors to only a bright white. The bright white light exploded, releasing a small shockwave throughout the location. Death jumped up with joy as Kendrick and Noldar took a moment to calm themselves down.

"Finally." Death said. "He should be able to speak with us."

"Speak with us?" Kendrick said. "Through that?"

"Why yes. What else would he speak through? ME?"

A low-pitched groan comes from the Holy Artifact. Death inching closer to the artifact with her ear. Kendrick and Noldar took several steps closer to the table. Trying to hear what Death is hearing.

"AH!" The voice said from the artifact.

"My god." Kendrick muted.

"By the power of Eden." Noldar said. "Its him."

"I know you're all there." The dark voice said. "I know who you are and what you desire."

"Brother. It's me. Your sister!"

"I know it's you. I sensed your presence from the very moment you and the Trickster God took these artifacts from their previous location. Where you killed those agents that were present in the laboratory."

"Wait, you can see us too?" Kendrick said.

"I can see a lot of things from this prison. Something that Harold Vosloo failed to understand. This prison of an artifact is not designed for eternity. I am only in here for a moment and then shall I be released in full."

"But, brother. I want to release you now."

"That will not work, my sister. You cannot change what has already been written. A prophecy cannot be undone. I have a time to be in here and I have a time to be released. When I am released, you'll know first-hand. The world will learn of it afterwards."

"What about helping us in our current cause?" Noldar said. "Giving us our desires as your sister promised us."

"Oh. I can give you the desires of your heart from inside this prison. My power has no limits beyond this universe. I was one of the first entities to exist at the dawn of this physical realm. I have been on countless wars amongst angels, gods, and cosmics. I once ruled this earth for one thousand years after I won it in battle."

"My brother knows his power."

"To gain the desires you seek so much, you must first travel to the city of Retropolis. Bring these artifacts along with you and place them in the middle of the city. When that is done, you will see something come from above you. That will be my first gift to you and a sign that your desires are near to you."

"What is coming from the sky?" Kendrick said. "If I may ask of that."

"What will come from the sky is an early present from me to the three of you. Take care of it well. For if you do not, you may not again receive such a present from me ever again in this lifetime."

"Far enough." Noldar said. "When do we leave for Retropolis?"

"Leave now. Place the artifacts in the middle of the city and the rest will follow. Do you understand?"

"Yes, my brother. We understand you."

"Good to hear. Now go and do what you must."

The voice vanished from the artifact as the light surrounded it has evaporated as well. Death looked at Kendrick and Noldar, smiling.

"So, let's take a trip."

The team continued fighting the Beast. The small town nearly decimated from the battle after The Beast slammed The Powerman and Theus through its buildings. Nano Man is still laid on the ground. His suit can no longer battle the Beast. Its power has decreased from the strength of the Beast. The Swordman and Norland run toward Beast.

"I'll take the front." The Swordman said. "You take the back."

"Agreed."

The Swordman took his sword and swiped the stomach of The Beast, slowing him down a bit, but increasing his strength. The Beast knocked Swordman through a window to the side as Norland jumped onto Beast's back.

'Guess I'll try this again!" Norland said.

The Beast grabbed Norland by his head and threw him to the ground, stomping on him. The Powerman flew over toward Beast, punching him in the face and kneeing him in his jaw.

Theus rammed Beast with his shoulder and slammed his hammer across The Beast's head, knocking him to his knees.

"He's down to his knees!" Theus said. "We're almost about to win this gruesome bout!"

"Be careful." The Swordman said. "Do not take his slowing down for a complete weakness. We must continue to do such until he falls out or transforms back into Mr. Brock."

"What of his mind control?"

"Leave that to me. My sword was able to withstand Theus' hammer. The sword will also be able to break the mind control that has been placed onto him."

"How are you going to do it?"

"With a swipe of the sword to the forehead."

"We'll have to keep him down for that."

"See that you do."

The team, except Nano Man starts to combat The Beast head on. The Beast breaks out of their attacks. Roaring in their faces as he punches and kicks them across the road and town. The Beast turned and sees Powerman flying toward him. Roaring, Beast runs to Powerman with his fist approaching.

"You want to do this I see." The Powerman said, raising up his own fists.

The fists of Powerman and Beast, collide, destroying the remaining buildings of the small town. Both are pushed by back the strength of their power. Nano Man notices Beast, beginning to pass out. Tired of the constant fighting.

"Now is the time, Swordman." Nano Man said.

"I see him."

The Beast slowly stood up as Theus released a lightning bolt atop The Beast' head, electrocuting him. Powerman fired out his lightning vision to Beast's head. Norland conjured a lightning bolt, that struck Beast in his head. The Swordman ran toward The Beast with his sword in front.

"This is now over."

The Swordman swiped the sword against Beast' forehead. A small amount of green mist fell from the wound on Beast's forehead as Theus evaporated it with a lightning bolt from his hand.

"That mist is Noldar's power." Theus said. "I could feel it within my veins."

The Beast fell to the ground, passed out and slowly transforming back into Brock. Who's knocked out. The team stood over him.

"Well, the battle is done." The Powerman said.

"We need to take him back to the hoverbase." The Swordman said. "We also must find out where they are."

The Swordman pressed a button on his wrist, calling out the Swordwing, which he placed Brock in the passenger side and Nano Man and Norland behind him. Flying from the small town to the hoverbase with Powerman and Theus flying behind him. Making it back to the hoverbase, Nader and Agent Mara took Brock to a secure room where he could rest up. Hawke was taken to another lab, where he could fix his armor. Nader walked up to Swordman and Norland.

"Do you have any clue where Death, Noldar, or Kendrick are?"

"We do not." Norland said. "That's why we came here to see if you guys had anything."

"We don't have nothing. Not even a small trace of where they possibly could be."

Agent Mara ran toward Nader as if she was racing on a track team. Nader turned to her, looking at her facial expression. Swordman and Norland also could tell that something was going on.

"Sir, you need to see this right now."

They followed her to the main area of the hover base. Where on the monitors, Death, Noldar, and Kendrick at Retropolis with the two artifacts in the middle of the city. Traffic is jammed around them with civilians screaming at them to move out of the roads. The artifacts glow and the sky exploded. Terrifying everyone, a portal opened from the sky. Death smiled.

"He sent them." She said.

"Who's them?" Kendrick said.

"Must be his army." Noldar said.

From the portal arrive a large army of cloaked figures riding on hover vehicles and dark winged horses with fire in their eyes and fire for manes. The figures' heads are covered with a black mask and hood. The army descended upon Retropolis where they began killing civilians and destroying the city.

"The hell is going on?" Nader said.

"They opened a portal to Helven." said The Swordman.

"Helven?" Norland said. "You meant Heaven, right?"

"No. They are the army of Helven. Helven is the realm where Death's brother resided and continues to rule over. That army is his own."

"Looks like you know where to find them now." Mara said.

"We're going to head there now and finish this." said The

Swordman.

Nader nodded as they leave the main section. The Swordman walked into the laboratory where Hawke was rebuilding his armor.

"We're going to Retropolis to stop them. We'll need you."

"I know. I'll be on my way. Don't wait up for me."

"We won't. Trust me."

The Swordman flew out in the Swordwing, Norland took a hoverjet, and Powerman and Theus flew from the hoverbase toward Retropolis. Hawke realized that he could not fight in the armor. He nodded, placed the armor on and returned to his Nano-Bunker. Inside, he placed the destroyed armor down and approached the closet. Searching through the armored exosuits, he found one and nodded.

"This one will surely do well."

Visiting Retropolis was both Stephanie Vale and Alex Havens from Enigma City. They stood close to the city, with Alex taking photos of the Helvish army surrounding the city and coming out of the dark portal above.

"Wondering when he'll show up." Alex said.

"Who?"

"The Powerman. You know he's going to be here."

"I could highly doubt that."

"He has to coming. This kind of stuff needs his help."

"This city has The Swordman to assist them. They don't need The Powerman to help them."

"We both know The Swordman is just a myth. Kind of like those fairy tales that we read so much of when we're children. He's one of those."

"You're sure about that?"

"I'm positive about it. There is no Swordman."

From above them flies pass the Swordwing, the hoverjet,

Powerman, and Theus. Flying toward the city and portal. Alex was stunned. Stephanie showed a faint smile toward him.

"Ok. I saw The Powerman. But, was that a flying sword as well?"

"I don't know, Alex. As you just said, The Swordman doesn't exist."

They arrived at the site of the artifacts. Exiting the Swordwing and hoverjet, they approached Death and Noldar. Kendrick was nowhere to be seen.

"Shut down the portal, Death." said The Swordman.

"No. I'm not going to do that."

"You will." Norland said. "Shut it down."

"Wow. Aren't you a bold one, Commander Norland. Giving orders where it isn't your place to give them."

"Where's Kendrick?" The Powerman said.

"I'm over here!" Kendrick said from behind them, wearing a white and gray armored suit.

"He dressed up for this." Norland said.

"He was prepared for what could come."

"As you can see, I'm ready for this fight you've brought to us." Noldar gazed around them and the sky.

"I'm noticing your armored friend is missing." Noldar said. "Did the Beast kill him before you managed to break my control over him?"

"Noldar, the time for your little games are over." Theus said. "This is the end for your schemes!"

"I think not, Son of Eden."

From the sky, the Helvish army came down, attacking the team. They fought back against them but were surrounded by even more Helvish soldiers. Kendrick ran toward Powerman, screaming as he punched him across the street, falling onto empty cars.

"I've been waiting to do that." Kendrick said. "Now to kill

you with my own two hands!"

The Swordman swiped the sword against the Helvish soldiers, cutting their heads and limbs off. Norand fought against them with spears, punches, and kicks. Theus and Noldar began to fight each other, taking the battle into the air. Swordman and Norland stood back to back as the Helvish army was approaching them from both sides.

"Where the hell is Hawke?" Norland said.

"He's on his way."

A series of energy beams come falling from the sky. Killing the soldiers as Nano Man landed onto the street, wearing a newly upgraded armor. Somewhat bulkier than the previous one. Nano Man approached Swordman and Norland, still surrounded by the Helvish army.

"What did I seem to miss?" Nano Man said.

"Them." said The Swordman.

The Helvish soldiers screamed at The Swordman, Nano Man, and Norland.

"Let's finish this." The Swordman said.

VII

WORLD'S PRODIGIOUS HEROES

The Swordman, Nano Man, and Commander Norland fight the Helvish Army on the Retropolis streets as The Powerman fights against the armored Kex Kendrick, along with Theus and Noldar fighting each other with hammer and spear in the sky. Death stood back, protecting the artifacts from the heroes on the ground.

"You do not need to oversee the artifacts, sister."

"But, they'll come and close the portal."

"I will handle the portal from here. Aid your partners against the ones who seek to destroy your plans."

"I will, my brother."

Death walked away from the artifacts as a force field grew from out of the ground, covering both artifacts from the fighting around them. Nano Man shoots out missiles from his forearms as the Helvish soldiers.

"When did you get missiles?" Norland said.

"I've always had them. But, this exosuit can carry so much more than the previous one."

"It's bulkier than the slimmer one." The Swordman said.

"But, its stronger and able to withstand powerful blows."

While fighting the soldiers, Death ran toward them, throwing death crosses at them. The Swordman dodged the crosses with his sword, staring at Death. Norland and Nano Man dealt with the soldiers. Death opened her arms, laughing.

"Come and get me, Swords!"

Swordman ran toward Death, swiping his sword at her as she dodged the coming swipes. Death kicked Swordman in the leg as he elbowed her in the face. Grabbing her coat, he tossed her across the road.

"Ouch!" She said.

"You brought this on yourself."

The Swordman walked toward her, he went to stomp her head into the road, she moved out of his boot's way as it hit the concrete. She ran and kicked him in the face and tripped him over with her legs. The Swordman fell to the ground as she jumped on top of him with a death cross in her hand. She goes to stab him in his chest, quickly he grabbed her arm.

"Come on. I want to do it!"

"You won't get the pleasure of killing me."

"But, I will one way or another!"

"Not today."

The Swordman hit Death in her head with his forehead and kicked her in the chest. She backed up as Swordman stood to his feet. She went to lunge at him, but she is caught by a rope, which surrounded her and pulled her back. Swordman looked to see where the rope came from and atop a nearby bank, wearing his gold archery uniform with his hood, Q-Arrow stood, saluting Swordman.

"I told you I would come!" Q-Arrow said.

"The rope gave it away!"

"It did not!"

Q-Arrow continued to fire arrows at the Helvish soldiers that were approaching him. Smiling as the arrows hit the soldiers, knocking them from the sky and collapsing on the road.

"I love this job."

On the ground, a motorcycle appears and riding on it is John Terror, shooting at the Helvish soldiers with a pair of machine guns. Terror stopped near Swordman and nodded.

"On my own time it seems." Terror said.

"You love to make an entrance."

"What do you need me to do?"

"Help us take out these soldiers on the streets."

"What about the ones in the air?"

"The Powerman and Theus will deal with them."

"I will too." Nano Man said. "You guys keep the ground soldiers in your sights. I'll assist with the aerial ones."

Nano Man flew up in the air, crashing into one of the Helvish hover vehicles, grabbing the soldiers who was riding on it and dropping him to the ground. On the ground, a pair of citizens were trapped inside a store, surrounded by Helvish soldiers. From the doors burst Dameon Mason, known as the Bionic Rage. Rage fought the soldiers, killing them with his bionic arms. Assisting the civilians to escape, The Swordman spotted him coming from the store.

"Good to see you've come." The Swordman said.

"I only came to help the people." Rage said. "That is all."

They nodded before going separate ways in the city.

The Powerman is being manhandled by Kendrick, as the two are fighting inside an office building.

"You believed that you could not be stopped?!" Kendrick said. "I'm a mortal man and I'm destroying you!"

"Take off the suit and let's see what you become of."

"Nah. I'm not listening to your little demands, 'Chosen Son'! I'm going to kill you right here, then the world will know you heroes are nothing but false gods."

"False gods?" The Powerman said with his eyes glowing gold.

The Powerman slowly hovered above Kendrick. Staring at him with anger.

"Allow me to show you what a real god can do."

The Powerman speared Kendrick through the building to the outside. Kendrick stood up as Powerman slowly appeared from the smoke of the falling walls.

"I am above what you are, Kex Kendrick. I am a titagod."

The Powerman punches Kendrick in his chest, pushing him through the Helvish soldiers. The Powerman went through them as if they were nothing but a wooden wall. Kendrick fired some missiles toward Powerman, though they had no effect on him.

"Your mortal weapons won't have an effect on me."

"What is happening?! I prepared for this moment!"

"You didn't prepare enough."

Powerman rammed his fist into the chest of Kendrick's suit, pulling out its power source. Kendrick fell to the ground as Powerman ripped the armor from his body, leaving on scraps of metal laying around the street.

"You've lost, Kendrick."

"I still have the portal open. I haven't lost yet."

Powerman looked at the portal and looked toward the covered artifacts. He flew toward them as Kendrick laid on the ground. Staring at the force field, Powerman punched it, but the field jolted a bolt of energy, knocking Powerman down across the roadway. Nano Man flew down toward the artifacts and fired a set of beams, having no effect on the force field.

"What is that force field made of?" The Powerman said.

"From what my helmet is describing. Made up of ancient magic."

"Its Negonic matter." The Swordman said walking toward them fighting soldiers.

"Negonic matter?"

"It's the Helvish aura. Created by Death's brother himself."

"So, how do we get through this force field?"

"I'm not sure just yet."

From the portal came a loud scream. The team looked up and sees a large monster coming from the portal. Appeared to be a mixture of a snake and shark as it flew down from the portal and toward them. The monster screamed as it rammed through buildings and toward the team. They stood their ground.

"How are we going to deal with that?" Norland said.

"With all our might."

From behind them comes a roar. They turned around to see The Unstoppable Beast landed behind them and jumped up toward the monster. The beast latched onto the monster's head, pulling it across the buildings.

"I did not see that coming." Nano Man said. "The Beast on our side."

"At least he's on our side."

The Beast stood atop the monster's head and smashed it to the ground. The Beast roared as he jumped back toward the team. He stared at them as they prepared to face him again.

"You don't want to do this." The Swordman said.

"We don't need to have another fight, Mr. Brock." Norland said. "Help us close this portal."

The Beast stared and later nodded as he walked toward the artifacts. Shoving Helvish soldiers out of his way. The Beast punched the field, but it had no effect. He continued to punch it and it still stood.

"Still not working." Norland said.

"Give it some time, Commander." Nano Man said. "Something will pull through."

Up in the sky, Theus and Noldar continue to battle each other. Hammer smashing against spear. Noldar laughed during their battle. Theus grabbed Noldar by his helmet and kicked him down to the roof of a building. Theus landed on the roof, walking toward Noldar.

"Don't you see what you're up against, Son of Eden?!"

"What do I not see?"

"True power. Real power from someone who can kill you and kill Eden."

"I will not allow you to possess such power!"

Noldar went to stab Theus with the spear, but Theus slammed the hammer atop the spear, breaking it in Noldar's hand. As the shreds of the spear fall to the roof, Theus kicked Noldar in the chest and picked him up with one arm, slamming him down and placed his foot on his throat.

"You've lost, Trickster God."

"The portal is still open. I haven't lost completely yet."

"Be that as it may."

Theus kicked Noldar in the face, knocking him out as he flew down to the artifacts where the others were. Coming down, Theus saw The Beast and ran toward him.

"This monster wants to fight again?!"

"No!" The Swordman said. "He's here to help us."

Theus saw The Beast punching the force field continually. Nano Man fired beams of energy as well.

"I will assist you." said Theus. "Allow me."

Theus flew up and shot down a lightning bolt atop the artifacts. Struggling to hold it against the force field, the field fired the lightning bolt back toward Theus, knocking him down. The Swordman looked around, seeing Q-Arrow, Terror, and Bionic Rage fighting the Helvish soldiers behind them. The Swordman looked at his sword and looked at the artifacts.

"My sword has power. Yet, I do not know how much power."

The Swordman walked toward the artifacts, telling the others to move away from the artifacts. Swordman raised up his sword and swiped the force field. The field slowly tampered away for a bit. Realizing it, Swordman shoved his sword through the force field, opening it.

"Grab the artifacts!" The Swordman said.

Norland ran over and grabbed the artifacts as Swordman removed his sword. The force field died, and the portal closed, sucking up the remaining Helvish soldiers that were alive back into their previous location. All that remained were the dead Helvish soldiers on the streets. Q-Arrow, Terror, and Bionic Rage walked over toward them with Death and Kendrick in tow. Theus returned to the rooftop and grabbed the unconscious Noldar, bringing him down to the street.

"It appears that we've won." Norland said.

"So it has." said The Swordman.

"This sucks!" Death said.

The saving of the city is broadcasted on the news across the world. With nearly every country witnessing the heroes for the first time. Calling the heroes, 'The Resistance'.

After several days, the city of Retropolis was being slowly repaired of its damages due to the battle. The Swordman returned Death back to Pegasus Prison, Kex Kendrick was sentenced to prison for an undisclosed amount of time, was posted out on bail. Theus took Noldar back to Eragard for his judgment.

Within the T.I.T.A.N. Headquarters base, Nader sat down at a table with Kenari, Hawke, Norland, Theus, and Powerman.

"I have to thank the five of you for saving the world."

"We did what we had to do." Kenari said.

"So, I will ask, are we being paid for this?" Hawke said. "It's just a question that's been on my mind lately."

"Why would we pay you?"

"Because I almost died out there. The Beast nearly killed me.

So did Noldar and this guy over here."

Theus laughed.

"The challenge of combating you was an honor. Though you are not dead. That is an honor in of itself."

"Funny." Hawke said. "Hope you laugh about it for days."

"I might."

"What of those other three that aided you guys? Q-Arrow, Terror, and Rage?"

"They're handling their own business it seems." Kenari said. "They'll come when they're needed."

"Where did Mr. Brock go?" Norland said.

"He's somewhere secluded." Nader said. "He'll be just fine."

They stand up from the table, leaving the office. Nader stopped Kenari and looked at him. The team also stopped.

"If we ever have a threat such as this or even bigger, we can count on you five to come and stop it?"

The office was quiet.

"We will unite if the threat is one of planetary or universal matter." Kenari said. "Right now, we have our own separate business to handle."

Theus walked outside and disappeared through a wormhole. Norland left on a motorcycle. The Powerman flew away, heading back to his fortress. Hawke entered his silver Lamborghini, driving away. Kenari walked out of the base and from above came the Swordwing. He entered it and flew away. Nader watched as the five heroes left from the base. He nodded.

"*The Resistance is Born.*"

ABOUT THE AUTHOR

Ty'Ron W. C. Robinson II is the author of several works of fiction. Including the *Dark Titan Universe Saga* series (*Dark Titan Knights, The Resistance Protocol, Tales of the Scattered, Tales of the Numinous, Day of Octagon*) and *The Haunted City Saga* series. Also of other books (*Lost in Shadows, Hod, The Book of The Elect, Symbolum Venatores, etc.*) and One-Shot short stories More information pertaining to the author and stories can be found at darktitanentertainment.com.